全新！NEW
GEPT

（興、許秀芬 —— 著

# 全民英檢

中高級

## 寫作&口說 題庫解析

新制修訂版

全書MP3一次下載

「iOS系統請升級至iOS 13後再行下載，
此為大型檔案，建議使用WIFI連線下載，以免佔用流量，
並確認連線狀況，以利下載順暢。」

全民英語能力分級檢定測驗（簡稱全民英檢）分為五級，高級、優級目前報考人數較少，一般實際運用仍以初級、中級、中高級為主流。以下簡單介紹這三個級別的內容。

## 1. 測驗項目

| 級別 | 初試通過標準 | 複試通過標準 |
|------|------------|------------|
| 初級<br>Elementary | 聽力&閱讀：兩項測驗成績總和達160分，且其中任一項成績不低於72分 | 寫作：70分<br>口說：80分<br>（各項滿分為100分） |
| 中級<br>Intermediate | 聽力&閱讀：兩項測驗成績總和達160分，且其中任一項成績不低於72分 | 寫作：80分<br>口說：80分<br>（各項滿分為100分） |
| 中高級<br>High-Intermediate | 聽力&閱讀：兩項測驗成績總和達160分，且其中任一項成績不低於72分 | 寫作：80分<br>口說：80分<br>（各項滿分為100分） |

## 2. 綜合能力說明

| 級別 | 綜合能力說明 |
|------|------------|
| 初級 | 具有基礎英語能力，能理解和使用淺易日常用語。（英語能力相當於國中畢業者） |
| 中級 | 具有使用簡單英語進行日常生活溝通的能力。（英語能力相當於高中畢業者） |
| 中高級 | 英語能力逐漸成熟，應用的領域擴大，雖有錯誤，但無礙溝通。（英語能力相當於大學非英語主修系所畢業者） |

## 3. 分項能力說明

| | 初級 | 中級 | 中高級 |
|---|---|---|---|
| 聽力 | 能聽懂與日常生活相關的淺易談話，包括價格、時間及地點等。 | 在日常生活中，能聽懂一般的會話；能大致聽懂公共場所廣播、氣象報告及廣告等。在工作時，能聽懂簡易的產品介紹與操作說明。能大致聽懂外籍人士的談話及詢問。 | 在日常生活中，能聽懂社交談話，並能大致聽懂一般的演講、報導及節目等。在工作時，能聽懂簡報、討論、產品介紹及操作說明等。 |
| 閱讀 | 可看懂與日常生活相關的淺易英文，並能閱讀路標、交通標誌、招牌、簡單菜單、時刻表及賀卡等。 | 在日常生活中，能閱讀短文、故事、私人信件、廣告、傳單、簡介及使用說明等。在工作時，能閱讀工作須知、公告、操作手冊、例行的文件、傳真、電報等。 | 在日常生活中，能閱讀書信、說明書及報章雜誌等。在工作時，能閱讀一般文件、摘要、會議紀錄及報告等。 |
| 寫作 | 能寫簡單的句子及段落，如寫明信片、便條、賀卡及填表格等。對一般日常生活相關的事物，能以簡短的文字敘述或說明。 | 能寫簡單的書信、故事及心得等。對於熟悉且與個人經歷相關的主題，能以簡易的文字表達。 | 能寫一般的工作報告及書信等。除日常生活相關主題外，與工作相關的事物、時事及較複雜或抽象的概念皆能適當表達。 |
| 口說 | 能朗讀簡易文章、簡單地自我介紹，對熟悉的話題能以簡易英語對答，如問候、購物、問路等。 | 在日常生活中，能以簡易英語交談或描述一般事物，能介紹自己的生活作息、工作、家庭、經歷等，並可對一般話題陳述看法。在工作時，能進行簡單的答詢，並與外籍人士交談溝通。 | 在日常生活中，對與個人興趣相關的話題，能流暢地表達意見及看法。在工作時，能接待外籍人士、介紹工作內容、洽談業務、在會議中發言，並能做簡報。 |

※測驗詳細介紹及報考資訊，請至全民英檢網 www.gept.org.tw 查看。

# CONTENTS

## 目録

## NEW GEPT
### 全新!全民英檢中高級 寫作&口說題庫解析

# 全民英寫作口說應考當天的注意事項

☆當天須攜帶的物品

□有效身分證件：中華民國身分證（或有效期限內的護照、駕照）正本。國中生可用：中華民國身分證、有效期限內的護照正本、印有相片之健保IC卡正本。外籍人士可用：有效期內的台灣居留證正本。

□自行列印的考試通知

□普通黑色鉛筆或藍／黑色原子筆、橡皮擦、修正帶

☆當天應試前的準備與注意事項

1. 以鉛筆作答者，請準備兩枝以上削尖的鉛筆或自動筆，因為考試開始後不可能有時間做削鉛筆的動作。以原子筆作答者，請準備兩枝以上的黑／藍色原子筆，並事先確認不會中途斷水，以防止因沒水而無法完成考試。

2. 務必提早到考場，給自己充裕時間確認貼在入口處／走廊上自己的考試教室與座位，以及做考前的複習，以免在快到測驗的時間時，不但要跟別的考生擠著確認自己的教室／座位，若遇到特殊情況（例如當天臨時換教室）也沒有足夠的時間應對。

3. 在測驗教室前排隊等候時，請利用時間保持英文思考的環境。一般到了考試現場，許多考生的習慣往往就是開始用中文聊天，這其實會扼殺自己的考試能力，因為在寫作／口說測驗中，直接以英文的思考邏輯來答題，表達出來的內容才最為流暢。因此，建議在入場前閱讀（或朗讀）英文的文章、句子，也可以聽英文廣播，來掌握英文的思考結構與流暢度。

4. 在進入考場之前，先把有效證件、准考證，以及相關文具都先準備好，取消所有電子儀器的鬧鈴設定，並將手機關機，以便於入場後能迅速將不需帶入座位之物品擺至測驗教室的前方地板上，並馬上找到自己的座位。

5. 為了讓口說測驗順利進行，在正式考試前考務人員會要求你檢查錄音設備，此時務必詳細檢查你的耳機、錄音設備是否都正常，而且不會干擾到你的答題，否則因錄音設備而影響到考試成績，是很冤枉的。

# 第一回　寫作能力測驗答題注意事項

1. 本測驗共有兩部分。第一部分為中譯英，第二部分為引導寫作。測驗時間為 **50 分鐘**。

2. 請利用試題紙空白處及背面擬稿，但正答務必書寫在「寫作能力測驗答案紙」上。在答案紙以外的地方作答，不予計分。

3. 第一部分中譯英請在答案紙第一頁開始作答，第二部分引導寫作請自答案紙第二頁起作答。

4. 作答時請勿隔行書寫，請注意字跡應清晰可讀，並請保持答案紙之清潔，以免影響評分。

5. 未獲監試人員指示前，請勿翻閱試卷。

6. 測驗時，不得在考試通知或其他物品上抄題，亦不得有傳遞、夾帶小抄、左顧右盼或交談等違規行為。

7. 意圖或已經將試卷攜出試場者，五年內不得報名參加本測驗。請人代考者，連同代考者，三年內不得報名參加本測驗。

8. 測驗結束時，須立即停止作答，在原位靜候監試人員收回全部試卷及答案紙，清點無誤後，宣佈結束始可離場。

9. 應試者入場、出場及測驗中如有違反上列規則或不服監試人員之指示者，監試人員得取消其應試資格並請其離場，且作答不予計分。

# 全民英語能力分級檢定測驗
## GENERAL ENGLISH PROFICIENCY TEST

## High-Intermediate Level Writing Test

### Part I: Chinese-English Translation (40%)

Translate the following Chinese passage into an English passage, and write your answer on the Writing Test Answer Sheet.

在社交媒體的時代，我們在網路上似乎沒有隱私。當我們在線上分享我們所想和所做的事時，我們的個人資訊可能被收集並且被用於有益和有害的方式。舉例來說，社交媒體網站使用我們的個人資訊來推薦我們可能有興趣的內容，而犯罪者可以藉由看我們發表過的照片來追蹤我們去過的地方。所以，我們需要小心注意我們在社交媒體上發表什麼。畢竟，分享我們生活的部分和分享全部是有所不同的。

### Part II: Guided Writing (60%)

Write an essay of **150~180 words** in an appropriate style on the following topic. Write your answer on the Writing Test Answer Sheet.

Road running has increased in popularity in recent years. More and more people are taking part in road running events whether as a competition or just a sport. In your essay, you should
(1) provide reasons for the popularity of road running, and
(2) discuss the benefits of such events.

# 全民英語能力檢定測驗

## 中高級寫作能力測驗答案紙

第一部分請由第 1 行開始作答，勿隔行書寫。第二部分請翻至第 2 頁作答。

1 _____

_____

_____

_____

5 _____

_____

_____

_____

_____

10 _____

_____

_____

_____

_____

15 _____

第二部分請翻至第 2 頁作答。

1

5

10

15

20

25

30

35

40

45

50

55

60

# 第一回　口說能力測驗答題注意事項

1. 本測驗問題由耳機播放，回答則經麥克風錄下。分回答問題、看圖敘述與申述題三部份，時間共約 20 分鐘，連同口試說明時間共需約 50 分鐘。

2. 第一部份回答問題的題目只播出一次，聽完題目後請立即回答。第二部份看圖敘述有 30 秒的思考時間及 1 分 30 秒的答題時間；第三部份申述題分別有 1 分 30 秒的思考時間及答題時間。思考時，請不要發出聲音。等聽到指示開始回答時，請針對圖片或申述題的題目在作答時間內盡量的表達。

3. 錄音設備皆已事先完成設定，請勿觸動任何機件，以免影響錄音。測驗時請戴妥耳機，將麥克風調到嘴邊約三公分處，依指示以適中音量回答。

4. 測驗進行間，不可以在試題紙以外任何物品上書寫與測驗相關之任何文字、符號，亦不可有傳遞、夾帶小抄、左顧右盼或交談等違規行為，否則作答不予計分。

5. 意圖或已將試題紙或試題影音資料攜出或傳送出試場者，視同侵犯本中心著作財產權，限五年內不得報名參加「全民英檢」測驗。請人代考者，連同代考者，三年內不得報名參加本測驗。

6. 測驗結束時，須立即停止作答，在原位靜候監試人員收回全部試題紙並清點無誤，等候監試人員宣布結束後始可離場。

7. 入場、出場及測驗中如有違反上列規則或不服監試人員之指示者，監試人員將取消您的應試資格並請您離場，且測驗成績不予計分，亦不退費。

# 全民英語能力分級檢定測驗

## GENERAL ENGLISH PROFICIENCY TEST

## High-Intermediate Level Speaking Test

**Please read the self-introduction sentence.**

My seat number is (座位號碼後 5 碼) , and my registration number is (考試號碼後 5 碼) .

### Part 1    Answering Questions

You will hear 8 questions. Each question will be spoken once. Please answer the question immediately after you hear it.

For questions 1 to 4, you will have 15 seconds to answer each question.

For questions 5 to 8, you will have 30 seconds to answer each question.

## Part II   Picture Description

Look at the picture, think about the questions below for 30 seconds, and then record your answers for 1½ minutes.

1. Where was this picture taken? What makes you think so?
2. What are the people doing? Why do you think they are doing this?
3. Have you or your friends done things like this? Tell me about your experience.
4. What are the benefits of this activity for the environment? Please explain.
5. If you still have time, please describe the picture in as much detail as you can.

## Part III    Discussion

Think about your answer(s) to the question(s) below for 1½ minutes, and then record your answer(s) for 1½ minutes. You may use your test paper to make notes and organize your ideas.

Many graduates struggle with low starting salary and high cost of living. How can fresh graduates manage to build up their savings under such an unfavorable situation? Do you think there is any way to solve this social issue? Please explain.

**Please read the self-introduction sentence again.**

My seat number is（座位號碼後 5 碼）, and my registration number is（考試號碼後 5 碼）.

# 複試 寫作測驗 解析

▶▶▶ 第一部分 中譯英 (40%)

將以下這段中文翻譯成英文。

在社交媒體的時代，我們在網路上似乎沒有隱私。當我們在線上分享我們所想和所做的事時，我們的個人資訊可能被收集並且被用於有益和有害的方式。舉例來說，社交媒體網站使用我們的個人資訊來推薦我們可能有興趣的內容，而犯罪者可以藉由看我們發表過的照片來追蹤我們去過的地方。所以，我們需要小心注意我們在社交媒體上發表什麼。畢竟，分享我們生活的部分和分享全部是有所不同的。

**翻譯範例**

In the age of social media, it seems [that] we have no privacy on the Internet. When we share what we think and do online, our personal information can be collected and used in both beneficial and harmful ways. For example, social media sites use our personal information to recommend content that we may be interested in, while criminals can track where we have been by looking at pictures we have posted. Therefore, we need to be careful about what we post on social media. After all, there is a difference between sharing parts of our life and [sharing] all of it.

**逐句說明**

1. 在社交媒體的時代，我們在網路上似乎沒有隱私。

   In the age of social media, it seems [that] we have no privacy on the Internet.

   • 「時代」在這裡翻譯成 age，但也可以用 time 來表達。

17

- 不管說成「社交媒體」還是「社群媒體」，英語都是 social media，這是許多文章中經常會出現的詞彙，所以一定要記得。

- 「似乎」用 seem 來表達。如果一時想不起「虛主詞 it + seems + that 子句」的句型，也可以寫成 we seem to have no privacy。

- [that] we have no privacy 也可以寫成 [that] we do not have privacy。

## 2. 當我們在線上分享我們所想和所做的事時，我們的個人資訊可能被收集並且被用於有益和有害的方式。

When we share what we think and do online, our personal information can be collected and used in both beneficial and harmful ways.

- 「我們所想和所做的事」用「複合關係代名詞 what + 主詞 + 動詞」來表達，或者也可以寫成 things [that] we think and do。

- online 其實就是 on the Internet 的意思，但為了避免和上一句重複而改變了表達方式，中文「在線上」也提示了這一點。

- 「個人資訊」是 personal information，表示和個人身分比較相關的一些重要資訊。

- 「被用於有益和有害的方式」在這裡是要表達好壞兩個方面都有可能，所以加上 both 會顯得比較自然。

## 3. 舉例來說，社交媒體網站使用我們的個人資訊來推薦我們可能有興趣的內容，而犯罪者可以藉由看我們發表過的照片來追蹤我們去過的地方。

For example, social media sites use our personal information to recommend content that we may be interested in, while criminals can track where we have been by looking at pictures we have posted.

- 「社交媒體」是 social media，那麼「社交媒體網站」就是 social media

site 了。這裡泛指各種社交媒體網站，所以加 -s，後面的 criminal 加 -s 也是同樣的理由。

- 因為句子前後內容分別是正面和負面的內容，所以把「而」理解成「然而」，使用連接詞 while 會比 and 來得好。

- 不要忘了「去過」是用 have been（曾經待過）而不是用 have gone to（已經離開到某個地方而沒有回來）表達。

- 雖然 have posted 改成簡單過去式 posted 似乎也沒錯，但因為是表達犯罪者針對我們「現在已經」發表過的照片來進行追蹤，所以選擇用現在完成式表達。

## 4. 所以，我們需要小心注意我們在社交媒體上發表什麼。

Therefore, we need to be careful about what we post on social media.

- 雖然中文寫的是「小心注意」，但不必刻意分成兩個詞來翻譯，只要用形容詞 careful 就能表達。careful 後面的介系詞除了 about 以外，也可以用 of 或 with。

- 「發表」在這裡用 post 來表達，我們平常所說的「po 文」就是從這個單字來的，也可以當名詞用，表示「一則發文」。除了 post 以外，也可以用動詞 publish 來表達。

## 5. 畢竟，分享我們生活的部分和分享全部是有所不同的。

After all, there is a difference between sharing parts of our life and [sharing] all of it.

- 「畢竟」的英文是 after all，沒有其他類似的說法，只能單獨記起來。

- 雖然這個句子也可以翻譯成 sharing parts of our life is different from sharing all of it，但如果想要更精確地表達「有所不同」（兩者之間有不一樣的地方），就可以使用這裡的 there is a difference between A and B 句型。請注意 difference 是可數名詞，所以要加冠詞 a。

依照以下主題，以適當的文體寫一篇 150~180 字的短文。

Road running has increased in popularity in recent years. More and more people are taking part in road running events whether as a competition or just a sport. In your essay, you should
(1) provide reasons for the popularity of road running, and
(2) discuss the benefits of such events.

近年路跑變得流行起來。有越來越多人參加路跑活動，不論是當成比賽或者只是運動。在你的短文中，你應該
(1) 提出路跑之所以流行的理由，並且
(2) 討論這種活動的好處。

**草稿擬定**

根據題目的提示，先設想大致上的文章結構，然後列舉自己想到的細節內容。這些內容可能沒辦法全部寫進文章，但可以作為寫作時的參考。

## 1. 路跑之所以流行的理由

→ 媒體的影響 the influence of the media
→ 宣傳 publicity
→ 適合各年齡層的 suitable for people of all ages
→ 初學者容易參與的 friendly to beginners
→ 不需要特別的裝備 no special gear required
→ 很多人一起跑更好（群眾效應）：比較有趣、有動力
crowd effect: more fun & motivation
→ 吸引人的獎品 attractive prizes

## 2. 活動的好處

→ 有益身心的 good for the body and mind
→ 結交新朋友（社交） make new friends (socialize)
→ 為慈善出一分力 do our part for charity

→ 成就感 sense of achievement

### 重點提示

- 中高級的引導寫作已經可以視為一篇完整的短文，所以必須分段。從字數來看，最少分兩段、最多分四段都是可行的。不過，本書為了示範如何寫出一段比較完整的論述，所以例文大多只有兩段，但每段的字數比較長，文章總長都達到上限 180 字左右。如果你覺得很難把段落寫長，可以考慮多分幾段，但每一段的論述一定要完整。

- 根據許多考生的經驗，文章超過字數上限並不是扣分的主因，但常犯文法、拼字錯誤的人要小心寫越多錯越多，扣分也越多。同樣的，字數寫得多也沒有加分效果，提升文章素質（遣詞用字有水準、文章連貫有條理、論述完整）才是高分之道。

- 由於時間和字數的限制，不可能把所有想到的論點都寫進去，你可以把類似的內容整合在一起。敘述一個論點時，請記得要有開頭的 topic sentence（主題句，通常是每個段落的第一或第二句）和 supporting sentences（後面用來支持論點的其他句子），才是一個完整的論述。

- 選擇要寫的論點時，必須考慮這些論點是否容易說明（以免寫不下去）、是否有說服力。

- 如果能使用一些慣用語，或者特別的表達方式，會有加分的效果。例如例文中提到的「所有年齡層」，可以用「people of all ages」或介系詞片語「from the elderly to children」來表達，展現你對文法及慣用表達方式的掌握程度。

- 「初學者容易參與」、「不需要特別的裝備」這兩個理由，可以藉由和其他運動的比較來證明，例如例文中是和網球、排球做比較。

- 在列舉幾個原因、理由之前，一個很簡單的開頭方式是「There are several reasons why...」，例如「There are several reasons why road running events are getting more and more popular.（路跑之所以越來越受歡迎，有幾個理由）」。這裡再提供另一種說法：「With many obvious benefits, road running is gaining in popularity.（由於許多明顯的好處，路跑現在越來越受歡迎）」。

①From a mini-marathon starting from 3km to a full 42km marathon, road running has become ②a highly popular sport in many cities around the world. There are several reasons for its popularity. First, ③running is an exercise suitable for people of all ages. In fact, ④it is not uncommon to see children and elder people taking part in road running events. Second, ⑤compared with competitive sports such as tennis or volleyball, running requires little equipment. Anyone can hit the road with their running shoes on. Last but not least, road running makes one feel connected to a community of ⑥like-minded people. Running with so many people pumps up your adrenaline and gets you all fired up.

Road running is actually more than a fad. It also helps participants to build up not only their muscles, but also stamina and willpower. In road running events, people around you ⑦serve as a source of motivation and encouragement. Besides increasing our personal sense of achievement, many such events also benefit society by raising funds for charities. That's what I call killing two birds with one stone.

從 3 公里開始的迷你馬拉松，到 42 公里的全程馬拉松，路跑已經成為全世界許多城市非常風行的運動。它的流行有幾個原因。首先，跑步是適合所有年齡層的運動。事實上，不難看見小孩和老年人參加路跑活動。第二，和網球、排球之類的競技性運動比起來，跑步需要的裝備很少。任何人只要穿上跑步鞋就可以上路。最後但也同樣重要地，路跑讓人感覺和一群志同道合的人有所連結。和這麼多人一起跑步，可以激發你的腎上腺素，讓你充滿熱情。

路跑其實不只是一時的流行而已。它也能幫助參加者鍛鍊肌肉、耐力和意志力。在路跑活動中，身邊的人是你動力和鼓勵的來源。除了增加我們個人的成就感以外，許多這類活動也因為募集慈善團體的基金而對社會有益。我會說這是一石二鳥。

**文法分析與替換表達方式**

① from... to...（從…到…）。如果你不知道路跑通常有幾公里，也可以寫成「From mini road runs to full-length marathons（從迷你路跑到全程馬拉松）」。如果要表達某事物可能的範圍，可以用 range from... to...（範圍從…到…）表達，例如「Road runs can range from 3km, for amateurs, to 42km for professionals.（路跑活動的〔長度〕範圍可以從業餘愛好者的 3 公里到職業選手的 42 公里）」。

② a highly popular sport（非常受歡迎的運動），highly 的意思和 very、really 相同。如果要表達「越來越受歡迎」，可以說「a sport that is gaining/rising in popularity」。

③ Running is suitable for people of all ages. 跑步適合各年齡層的人。
   ≒ Running caters to the needs of people of all ages.
      路跑能迎合各年齡層的人的需求。
   ≒ Whether young or old, people can take part in this event.
      不論老幼，人們都可以參加這項活動。
   ≒ Regardless of age or sex, everyone can join in the fun.
      不論年齡、性別，每個人都可以加入這好玩的活動。

④ it is not uncommon to see... 不難看見…（看見…並非不尋常）
   ≒ ... is quite a common sight …是很常見的景象
   ≒ it is not surprising to see... 看到…並不令人驚訝

⑤ compared with... 和…相比
   ≒ in contrast to... 相對於…（表示後面將提到的人事物性質不同或相反）

⑥ like-minded people 想法相同（志同道合）的人
   ≒ people with similar interests 有類似興趣的人
   ≒ people who share the same interest 有相同興趣的人

⑦ serve as a source of（充當…的來源）。serve as... 表示具有某個人或事物的功能。

⑧ 例文中道地的英文表達方式：
   hit the road 上路
   feel connected 感覺和別人在精神上有所連結、融入
   pump up your adrenaline 激發你的腎上腺素（使你興奮、有衝勁）
   all fired up 充滿熱情、激情的
   kill two birds with one stone 一石二鳥

# 複試 口說測驗 解析

▶▶▶ 第一部分 回答問題

> 你會聽到 8 個問題。每個問題會唸一次。請在聽到題目後立刻回答。第 1 到第 4 題,每題有 15 秒可以回答。第 5 到第 8 題,每題有 30 秒可以回答。

## 1 Do you have a driver's license? Why or why not?

**你有駕照嗎?為什麼?**

答題策略

1. 假如你有駕照,這題會很容易作答。你可以說你是什麼時候取得駕照的、你為什麼要去考駕照、考到駕照後有什麼好處。假設你沒有駕照,可以提到你預計什麼時候要去考。你也可以提到常在新聞上看到無照駕駛(drive without a license)的年輕人發生悲劇,所以你一定會等到有駕照才會開車。你甚至可以抱怨現在的停車位(parking spaces)比車子還貴,根本買不起,所以你不打算去考駕照,因為有了駕照就會有買車子的衝動。

2. 如果回答長度不夠的話,你也可以談談別人的意見來增加內容,例如「我的父母認為…」,說父親鼓勵你考駕照,但母親擔心你的安全,堅持要你坐捷運,不准你開車等等,但別忘了一定要先回答問題(你有沒有駕照),有多的時間才延伸其他內容。

回答範例 A

Yes, I do. Having a driver's license is absolutely necessary in my line of work. Sometimes I have to pick up clients at the airport or train station. On weekends, I can drive my family around.

是的，我有。在我的行業裡，擁有駕照是絕對必要的。有時候我必須開車到機場或車站接客戶。在週末，我可以開車載家人到處逛。

**回答範例 B**

No, I don't. Although I'm already eighteen years old, my mom insists that I'm too young to drive a car. I certainly hope she will change her mind in a year or two. Some of my friends drive to school. It's so cool.

不，我沒有。雖然我已經 18 歲了，但我媽堅稱我還太年輕不能開車。我真的希望她一兩年後會改變心意。我有些朋友開車上學。真的很酷。

|單字片語| **line of work** 行業 / **pick up** 開車接（某人）

## 2　What Chinese festival do you look forward to the most? Why do you like it?

你最期待什麼華人節日？你為什麼喜歡這個節日？

**答題策略**

1. 重大的華人節日有農曆新年、端午節和中秋節。用這三個比較安全，也有比較多的內容可以發揮。選擇其中一個節日後，可以敘述這個節日的主要活動，還有你喜歡這個節日的原因。
2. 如果要回答七夕（可以直接說成 Qixi「七夕」）的話，可以說「因為那是中式情人節（Chinese Valentine's Day）」，然後說那一天會做什麼情人節的活動。如果要解釋節日的由來，時間恐怕不夠用，而且難度太高，除非你曾經讀過關於傳統節日的英文介紹，不然可能會弄巧成拙。

**回答範例 A**

When it comes to Chinese festivals, my favorite has to be Mid-Autumn festival. It's a time when family members get together. I enjoy having a barbecue on that day. It's something I look forward to

第 1 回
第 2 回
第 3 回
第 4 回
第 5 回
第 6 回

every year.

説到華人節日，我最愛的一定是中秋節。這是家庭成員團聚的時刻。我喜歡在那天烤肉。那是我每年都期待的事。

Needless to say, it has to be Chinese New Year. It's a time when we have a family reunion. I get to see many relatives. The best part is getting lucky money in red envelopes.

不用説，那一定是農曆新年。這是我們家人團聚的時候。我能見到許多親戚。最棒的是能得到（紅包裡的）壓歲錢。

|單字片語| **have a barbecue** 烤肉 / **Needless to say, ...** 不用說，當然 / **reunion** [ri`junjən] n. 重聚，團聚 / **get to do** （口語）有機會做⋯，能夠做⋯ / **the best part is...** （某件事物）最棒的一點是⋯

## 重點補充

重要傳統節日的名稱：

端午節 Dragon Boat Festival / 中秋節 Mid-Autumn Festival / 清明節 Tomb-sweeping Day / 中元節 Ghost Festival

## 3 Your friend is a police officer. Ask him about the challenges he faces when enforcing the law.
你的朋友是警察。問他在執法時遇到的困難。

## 答題策略

「你的誰是⋯問他一些問題」是固定會出的題型，雖然根據對方的職業來提問比較好，不過也有一些「萬能」的問題，適用於所有職業，例如：

What's your job like? I mean, what do you actually do?（你的工作是怎樣的？我的意思是，你實際上做什麼？）

Do you find the job stressful?（你覺得工作壓力大嗎？）

What is the most difficult thing about your job?（你工作最難的地方是什麼？）

Do you get a sense of satisfaction from your job?（你在工作中得到滿足感嗎？）

If you can choose your career again, will you do something else?（如果你可以重新選擇職業，你會做別的嗎？）

## 回答範例 A

Isn't it tough to be a police officer? From what I see on TV, your job must be really challenging. What do you think is the most dangerous part? Tell me honestly, did you ever feel afraid?

當警察不是很辛苦嗎？從我在電視上看到的，你的工作一定很有挑戰性（很困難）。你覺得最危險的部分是什麼？老實告訴我，你曾經感覺害怕嗎？

## 回答範例 B

Congratulations! You're a police officer now! So, how do you deal with people who break the law? Do you go tough on them, or do you try to reason with them?

恭喜！你現在是警察了！那麼，你怎麼處理違法的人呢？你會對他們很嚴厲，還是會試圖勸說他們呢？

|單字片語| **reason with** 規勸，勸說（某人）

### 重點補充

臨時想不出還要問什麼的情況下，只好來個「我好崇拜你」的橋段。

I'm really envious of you. What can I do to become a police officer just like you? Can you give me some advice?（我很羨慕你。我要做什麼才能成為像你一樣的警察呢？你能給我一點建議嗎？）

**Your friend found a wallet. He intends to take the money in it. Persuade him not to do that.**

你的朋友發現了錢包。他想要拿裡面的錢。說服他不要那麼做。

**答題策略**

「勸誰不要…」也是經常出現的題型。開頭第一句應該表示你不認同對方的作法（例如以下的範例 A），或者直接說應該採取的其他行動（範例 B），然後說明你的立場，試圖說服對方。

回答範例 A

I don't think that's a good idea. I know you didn't steal the wallet from anyone, but it still feels like stealing. You know, taking something that doesn't belong to you.

我覺得那不是個好主意。我知道你不是偷別人的錢包，但感覺還是像在偷。你知道的，就是拿不屬於你的東西。

回答範例 B

Maybe we should leave the money in the wallet and take it to the police station. Look at the owner, he's about our age. I would be really grateful if someone returns to me something I lost.

或許我們應該把錢留在錢包裡，並且拿到警察局。你看錢包的主人，跟我們年紀差不多。如果有人把我弄丟的東西還我，我真的會很感謝。

|單字片語| **be about one's age** 跟某人年紀差不多

如果真的想不到反駁的理由，可以說「就是覺得不行」，例如：

If I were you, I wouldn't do that. It just feels wrong. Maybe you should reconsider.（如果我是你的話，我不會那麼做。感覺就是不對。或許你應該重新考慮。）

5  **What do you think are the reasons that social networking apps such as Facebook and Line are so popular nowadays?**

你覺得為什麼 Facebook 和 Line 之類的社交 app 現在這麼流行？

**答題策略**

1. 第五題開始作答時間增加為 30 秒。被問到一個現象的理由時，建議用「小作文」的方式進行口說。例如這一題，開頭可以先說這類 app 受歡迎的原因有幾個（There are several / a couple of reasons for their popularity.），然後用 First, ... Second, ... Last but not least, ... 的結構分別說明原因。在考試中很難在剛好 15 秒或 30 秒的時候說完，所以建議盡量說多一點，即使超過時間、錄音被切掉也沒有關係。

2. 如果一時想不到足夠的理由也沒關係，因為你應該也用過這些 app，所以你可以分享自己使用的經驗、通常用這些 app 做什麼（聯絡家人、分享美食和旅遊照片…）、使用時的感覺等等，都有助於增加回答的長度。

回答範例 A

There are a couple of reasons for the popularity of Facebook and Line. First, they allow users to keep in touch with their family and friends easily. Besides text messages, we can share pictures and even videos. These apps are user-friendly and convenient as long as you're connected to the Internet. On top of that, they're absolutely free. Personally, I spend hours each day using Facebook and Line.

Facebook 和 Line 的流行有幾個原因。首先，它們讓使用者能輕易和家人、朋友保持

聯絡。除了文字訊息，我們也能分享照片，甚至影片。只要你連上網路，這些 app 是很容易使用而且方便的。此外，它們完全免費。我個人每天會花幾個小時使用 Facebook 和 Line。

回答範例 B

As a matter of fact, most of my friends have Facebook accounts, and even my grandma is using Line. These social networking apps are really useful because they help people to stay in touch. We no longer have to send hand-written letters and wait for days to get a reply. Facebook and Line also come with games, so they can be used for entertainment. Personally, I use Facebook to search for information I'm interested in.

事實上，我的朋友大部分都有 Facebook 帳號，就連我奶奶也在用 Line。這些社交 app 真的很有用，因為它們幫助人們保持聯絡。我們不再需要寄手寫信，然後等好幾天才能得到回覆。Facebook 和 Line 也有遊戲，所以也可以作為娛樂使用。我個人使用 Facebook 搜尋我有興趣的資訊。

|單字片語| **social networking** 網路社交 / **keep/stay in touch** 保持聯絡 / **on top of that** 此外 / **personally** [ˈpɝsn̩lɪ] adv. 就我個人而言；親自，當面 / **account** [əˈkaʊnt] n. 帳戶，帳號

## 6 Do you think it is more effective to learn English at a language school than by yourself? Please explain.

你認為在語言補習班學英文比自己學有效嗎？請說明。

**答題策略**

對於這類二選一的題型，開頭可以選擇回答是或不是，然後再針對你的答案說明理由。但是，因為幾乎沒有構思答案的時間，所以如果一時想不到應該回答哪個，也可以像範例 B 一樣先說「it depends on...（取決於…）」，接著說自己的情況，在說明的同時回答自己屬於哪一種。不論如何，這一題最好的回答法是回想你自己學英文的情況，說明自己曾經使用過的學習方式，會

比較容易想到可以說的內容。除了自己的角度以外，如果還有時間的話，可以從不同人的立場和需求提出不同的看法。

## 回答範例 A

Frankly speaking, it's more effective to learn English at a language school than by myself. I have to admit that I lack motivation. I need someone to tell me what to do and when to do it. It's also more fun to study in a language school because I can meet new friends. If I run into problems with some words or sentences, I can ask the teacher for help .

老實說，在語言補習班學英文是比我自己學有效。我必須承認自己缺乏動力。我需要有人告訴我做什麼、何時去做。在語言補習班學習也比較有趣，因為我可以認識新朋友。如果我發現對某些單字或句子有困難，可以尋求老師的幫助。

## 回答範例 B

I guess it depends on the learner's personality and needs. For me, I prefer to study on my own because I can learn at my own pace. There are many self-study books that come with MP3 files. There are also many resources on the Internet. For example, I enjoy watching video lessons on YouTube. I can leave comments if I have doubts, and some helpful people will answer my questions.

我想這大概取決於學習者的個性和需求。對我來說，我偏好自學，因為可以用自己的步調學習。有很多附 MP3 檔案的自學書。網路上也有很多資源。例如，我很喜歡看 YouTube 上的教學影片。如果有疑問，我可以留言，有些熱心幫忙的人會回答我的問題。

---

【單字片語】 language school 語言學校；語言補習班 / motivation [ˌmotə'veʃən] n. 動機，積極性，幹勁 / run into 偶然遇到…；遭遇（困難等） / at one's own pace 用自己的步調 / leave a comment （在網路上）留言

關於學習方式的詞彙：

在家學習 home learning / 一對一家教 one-on-one tutoring

## 7 If you were choosing someone to date, what kind of people would you find attractive?

假設你在選擇約會的對象，你會覺得哪種人有吸引力？

**答題策略**

選擇交往的對象，可以從外貌、個性、工作等方面來思考，例如長得好看（good-looking）、身體健壯（fit）、隨和（easy-going）、善交際（sociable）、認真工作（hard-working）、有穩定的收入（have a stable income）等等。除了用形容詞描述以外，最好也能說明具體的特徵、事例、理由等等，這樣自然就能讓回答的內容變得充實了。

**回答範例** A

Well, I think appearance is the most important for me. I'm usually attracted to someone who has long hair and big eyes, just like my favorite singer Selena Gomez does. Besides appearance, I think it's also important that we have similar interests. If there's nothing in common between us, it will be difficult for us to have a good conversation.

嗯，我認為外貌對我而言是最重要的。我通常會被有長髮和大眼睛的人吸引，就像我最愛的歌手賽琳娜・戈梅茲一樣。除了外貌以外，我認為我們擁有類似的興趣也很重要。如果我們之間沒有共同點，就很難有良好的對話了。

第 1 回

第 2 回

第 3 回

第 4 回

第 5 回

第 6 回

I'd like to date someone who is gentle and caring because such kind of people make me feel relaxed and comfortable. Also, I hope he is willing to listen to different points of view. It's inevitable that people have different values, so I think it would be perfect if he could be as open-minded as I am and accept the differences between us.

我想和溫柔又關心別人的人約會，因為這種人讓我覺得輕鬆又自在。還有，我希望他願意聽不同的意見。人們難免會有不同的價值觀，所以我認為，如果他能和我一樣有開放的心態，並且接受我們之間的不同，那就完美了。

|單字片語| **open-minded** [ˋopənˋmaɪndɪd] adj. 心態開放的（願意接納不同的意見）

## 8 What are the advantages or disadvantages of traveling alone?
獨自旅行的好處或壞處是什麼？

### 答題策略

1. 因為題目中的連接詞是「or」，所以只要從好或壞的方面擇一說明就行了。當然，如果還有時間的話，也可以在最後稍微補充另一方面的觀點。
2. 獨自旅行的好處包括比較自由（have more freedom）、能和當地人交朋友（make friends with locals）、比較沒有壓力（less stressful）、建立自信（build self-confidence）等等。壞處則有住宿可能比較貴（accommodation may cost more）、可能不安全（might be unsafe）、會覺得寂寞（feel lonely）等等。

回答範例 A

Traveling alone helps us step out of our comfort zone. Without partners, we have to work out a solution ourselves when a problem arises. Also, we're more likely to talk with locals when we travel by ourselves, which means we have more chances to meet new friends and even build lasting global friendships. That would be an unforgettable experience in our life!

獨自旅行能幫助我們踏出舒適圈。因為沒有夥伴，所以當問題發生時，我們必須自己想出解決辦法。還有，我們自己旅行的時候也比較有可能和當地人交談，這意味著我們有更多機會遇見新朋友，甚至建立長久的國際友誼。那會是我們人生中很難忘的經驗！

### 回答範例 B

Personally, I don't like the idea of solo travel. Many unpredictable problems can occur while traveling, and it would be more difficult to solve them alone. For example, when our money or smartphones are lost during a trip, we may panic and have no idea what to do. However, if we travel with our family or friends, they can help us calm down and find a solution. That would make things easier for sure.

我個人不喜歡獨自旅行這個主意。旅遊時可能發生許多不可預測的問題，靠自己解決會比較困難。舉例來說，當我們的錢或者智慧型手機在旅行中遺失時，我們可能會驚慌失措，不知道該怎麼辦。不過，如果我們和家人或朋友一起旅行，他們可以幫助我們冷靜並且找到解決方法。那樣一定會讓事情變得比較簡單。

|單字片語| comfort zone 舒適圈 / work out a solution 想出解決辦法 / local [`lokl] n. 當地人 / personally [`pɝsnlɪ] adv. 就個人而言 / unpredictable [ˌʌnprɪ`dɪktəbl] adj. 不可預測的

▶▶▶ 第二部分 看圖敘述

請看照片，用 30 秒的時間思考以下問題，然後用 1 分半的時間錄下你的回答。

1. Where was this picture taken? What makes you think so?
2. What are the people doing? Why do you think they are doing this?
3. Have you or your friends done things like this? Tell me about your experience.
4. What are the benefits of this activity for the environment? Please explain.
5. If you still have time, please describe the picture in as much detail as you can.

1. 這張照片是在哪裡拍的？為什麼你這麼認為？
2. 這些人在做什麼？你認為他們為什麼要做這件事？
3. 你或你的朋友曾經做過像這樣的事嗎？告訴我你的經驗。
4. 這項活動對環境的好處是什麼？請說明。
5. 如果你還有時間，請盡量詳細描述這張照片。

1. 先敘述照片在哪裡拍攝，並舉證說明
2. 提到圖中的人物在做什麼
3. 針對人物的衣著和手持物品做出一些猜想
4. 自己是否做過這件事，或者曾經聽朋友說、看過新聞報導
5. 談論自己對於淨灘活動及垃圾問題的想法

回答口說題目時，雖然對於相關話題進行延伸討論有可能達到加分的效果，但最重要的還是回答題目中所提示的問題。如果只是想到什麼就說什麼，卻完全沒提到照片的內容，也沒有回答問題，反而會因為不合題意而降低得分。以本題而言，必須先說明圖片中的活動（淨灘）、自己是否做過這件事、淨灘對環境的好處，行有餘力才能繼續討論其他內容，例如海洋垃圾的問題、動物可能誤食垃圾、民眾在野外遊玩時如何避免製造垃圾等等。

We can see sand and sea in this picture, so I think it was taken on a beach. In the picture, there are four people carrying plastic bags, and they are picking up trash from the beach. Everyone is wearing a white T-shirt, so perhaps they're a group of volunteers. They're also wearing gloves so that they don't get hurt. It seems that they're participating in a beach cleaning activity. Actually, my school also asks its teachers and students to help clean up the beach nearby on Earth Day every year, so my classmates and I have done it several times. It's quite tough to carry all the trash under the sun, but as I saw many beachgoers happily helped us with the cleanup, I was deeply moved and felt that we were doing something meaningful. Removing trash not only makes beaches beautiful again, but also prevents animals from dying due to consuming plastic waste. However, compared to doing cleanups, I think it is more important not to pollute our environment with garbage in the first place. Wherever we go, whether to the beach or to the mountains, we should bring our own trash bags and not litter. It's also a good idea that we use reusable water bottles to reduce waste. As we can see in the picture, there are many plastic bottles left on the beach. Since plastic bottles are not biodegradable, they can stay in the environment forever. Therefore, we should cut the use of them when we can.

範例中譯

我們可以在這張照片裡看到沙子和海，所以我認為這是在海灘上拍的。在照片裡，有四個帶著塑膠袋的人，他們正在把海灘上的垃圾撿起來。每個人都穿著白色 T 恤，所以他們或許是一群志工。他們也戴著手套，好讓他們不會受傷。看起來，他們正在參加淨灘活動。事實上，我的學校也要求老師和學生每年在地球日幫忙清理附近的海灘，所以我的同學和我做過幾次。在太陽下帶著那堆垃圾很辛苦，但當我看到許多到海邊的人很樂意幫我們清理時，我非常感動，而且覺得我們在做有意義的事情。去除垃圾不但讓海灘再次變得美麗，也能防止動物因為吃下塑膠垃圾而死亡。不過，和進行清理比起來，我認為一開始就不要用垃圾污染環境比較重要。我們去任何地方的時候，不管是去海邊或是山上，我們都應該帶自己的垃圾袋，並且不要亂丟垃圾。使用可重複使用的水瓶來減少垃圾也是個好主意。就像我們在照片中可以看到的，海灘上遺留了許多塑膠瓶。因為塑膠瓶不是生物可降解的，所以可能永遠停留在環境中。所以，我們應該能減少使用就減少使用。

|單字片語| **beach cleaning (beach cleanup)** 淨灘 / **Earth Day** 地球日 / **beachgoer** [ˋbitʃͺgoɚ] **n.** 去海邊的人 / **consume** [kənˋsjum] **v.** 吃，喝 / **litter** [ˋlɪtɚ] **v.** 亂丟垃圾 / **reusable** [riˋjuzəbl] **adj.** 可重複使用的 / **biodegradable** [ˋbaɪodɪˋgredəbl] **adj.** 生物可降解的

> 請用 1 分半的時間思考你對於以下問題的答案，然後用 1 分半的時間錄下你的回答。你可以用測驗卷做筆記並整理你的想法。

Many graduates struggle with low starting salary and high cost of living. How can fresh graduates manage to build up their savings under such an unfavorable situation? Do you think there is any way to solve this social issue? Please explain.

**許多畢業生因為低起薪、高生活費而辛苦。在這種不利的情況下，剛畢業的學生可以怎樣累積儲蓄？你認為有方法可以解決這個社會問題嗎？請說明。**

【草稿擬定】

1. 對於畢業生的起薪少於三萬，生活消費卻相當高這個事實表示同情。
2. 解決方法為開源節流：一方面增加收入，另一方面減少支出。
3. 開源：升遷、加薪、兼差。節流：少購物。

【回答範例】

This is quite a complicated and sensitive issue. According to what I heard from the news, the starting salary for fresh graduates like me is less than thirty thousand NT dollars. With the high cost of living, especially in Taipei, the future for the younger generation looks bleak. Under such an unfavorable situation, there are only two ways for us to build up our savings. First, we should excel at what we do and learn as much as we can on the job. With experience and a positive attitude at work, we have a better chance of getting a raise or a promotion. If time permits, we can take a part-time job to increase our income. Three to five thousand dollars of extra income a month adds up to a significant sum in three to five years. Second, it is necessary that we cut down on our expenses and live below our means. To quote from a book I have read: "What you want is not what you need." We must tell the difference between something we simply desire and something we truly need. For example, we all want new shoes, watches, and clothes when we go shopping. In reality, we can often make do with what we already have instead of making new purchases. In conclusion, I don't expect the government to solve the problem. We can only depend on ourselves.

**範例中譯**

這是個相當複雜而棘手的問題。根據我從新聞中聽到的，像我一樣剛畢業的學生起薪不到三萬台幣。因為生活費高昂，尤其在台北，年輕一代的未來看起來沒有希望。在這樣不利的情況下，只有兩個方法可以讓我們累積儲蓄。首先，我們應該在職場上把我們做的事做得特別優異，而且盡可能多學習。有了經驗和積極的工作態度，我們就有比較好的機會可以獲得加薪或升職。如果時間允許的話，我們可以找兼職工作來增加收入。一個月三到五千元的額外收入，三到五年後可以累積成很大的總額。第二，我們有必要削減支出，並且量入為出。引用我讀過的一本書：「想要不等於需要」。我們必須分辨只是渴望的東西和真正需要的東西之間的差別。例如，我們購物時都想要新的鞋子、手錶和衣服。事實上，我們通常可以將就用已經擁有的東西，而不用買新的。總而言之，我並不期望政府解決這個問題。我們只能靠自己。

|單字片語| **starting salary** 起薪 / **build up one's savings** 累積儲蓄 / **unfavorable** [ʌnˋfevrəbl] adj. 不利的 / **sensitive** [ˋsɛnsətɪv] adj. 敏感的；棘手的 / **bleak** [blik] adj. 淒涼的，沒有希望的 / **excel at** 特別擅長做… / **on the job** 工作時 / **have a better chance of doing** 比較有機會能做… / **get a raise** 獲得加薪 / **if time permits** 時間允許的話 / **cut down on** 削減… / **live below one's means** 量入為出（生活在收入的標準以下） / **in reality** 實際上 / **make do with** 用…勉強度過

學習筆記欄

# 第二回　寫作能力測驗答題注意事項

第 1 回
第 2 回
第 3 回
第 4 回
第 5 回
第 6 回

1. 本測驗共有兩部分。第一部分為中譯英，第二部分為引導寫作。測驗時間為 **50 分鐘**。

2. 請利用試題紙空白處及背面擬稿，但正答務必書寫在「寫作能力測驗答案紙」上。在答案紙以外的地方作答，不予計分。

3. 第一部分中譯英請在答案紙第一頁開始作答，第二部分引導寫作請自答案紙第二頁起作答。

4. 作答時請勿隔行書寫，請注意字跡應清晰可讀，並請保持答案紙之清潔，以免影響評分。

5. 未獲監試人員指示前，請勿翻閱試卷。

6. 測驗時，不得在考試通知或其他物品上抄題，亦不得有傳遞、夾帶小抄、左顧右盼或交談等違規行為。

7. 意圖或已經將試卷攜出試場者，五年內不得報名參加本測驗。請人代考者，連同代考者，三年內不得報名參加本測驗。

8. 測驗結束時，須立即停止作答，在原位靜候監試人員收回全部試卷及答案紙，清點無誤後，宣佈結束始可離場。

9. 應試者入場、出場及測驗中如有違反上列規則或不服監試人員之指示者，監試人員得取消其應試資格並請其離場，且作答不予計分。

# 全民英語能力分級檢定測驗
## GENERAL ENGLISH PROFICIENCY TEST
## High-Intermediate Level Writing Test

## Part I: Chinese-English Translation (40%)

Translate the following Chinese passage into an English passage, and write your answer on the Writing Test Answer Sheet.

在渴望減重的人當中，有些人寧願嘗試各種藥，而不是改變自己的生活型態。醫師警告，來路不明的減肥藥丸可能極為有害，造成如腎臟損傷之類的副作用。減重最有效的方法是規律的運動和低卡路里飲食。它們相輔相成，其中一個少了另一個就沒有用。少了飲食習慣的改變，多少運動都會是徒勞無功的。

## Part II: Guided Writing (60%)

Write an essay of **150~180 words** in an appropriate style on the following topic. Write your answer on the Writing Test Answer Sheet.

As artificial intelligence (AI) develops and becomes more common in our daily lives, it is worried that some people, such as translators and accountants, will lose their jobs in the future. However, it is also predicted that the need to cooperate with AI will create new jobs. In your essay, you should
(1) discuss in what ways can AI assist or replace human workers, and
(2) share your thoughts about what will be required to survive in the job market.

# 全民英語能力檢定測驗
## 中高級寫作能力測驗答案紙

第一部分請由第 1 行開始作答，勿隔行書寫。第二部分請翻至第 2 頁作答。

1 _____

_____

_____

_____

5 _____

_____

_____

_____

_____

10_____

_____

_____

_____

_____

15_____

第二部分請翻至第 2 頁作答。

1 _____

_____

_____

_____

5 _____

_____

_____

_____

_____

10 _____

_____

_____

_____

_____

15 _____

_____

_____

_____

_____

20 _____

25

30

35

40

45

50

55

60

# 第二回　口說能力測驗答題注意事項

1. 本測驗問題由耳機播放，回答則經麥克風錄下。分回答問題、看圖敘述與申述題三部份，時間共約 20 分鐘，連同口試說明時間共需約 50 分鐘。

2. 第一部份回答問題的題目只播出一次，聽完題目後請立即回答。第二部份看圖敘述有 30 秒的思考時間及 1 分 30 秒的答題時間；第三部份申述題分別有 1 分 30 秒的思考時間及答題時間。思考時，請不要發出聲音。等聽到指示開始回答時，請針對圖片或申述題的題目在作答時間內盡量的表達。

3. 錄音設備皆已事先完成設定，請勿觸動任何機件，以免影響錄音。測驗時請戴妥耳機，將麥克風調到嘴邊約三公分處，依指示以適中音量回答。

4. 測驗進行間，不可以在試題紙以外任何物品上書寫與測驗相關之任何文字、符號，亦不可有傳遞、夾帶小抄、左顧右盼或交談等違規行為，否則作答不予計分。

5. 意圖或已將試題紙或試題影音資料攜出或傳送出試場者，視同侵犯本中心著作財產權，限五年內不得報名參加「全民英檢」測驗。請人代考者，連同代考者，三年內不得報名參加本測驗。

6. 測驗結束時，須立即停止作答，在原位靜候監試人員收回全部試題紙並清點無誤，等候監試人員宣布結束後始可離場。

7. 入場、出場及測驗中如有違反上列規則或不服監試人員之指示者，監試人員將取消您的應試資格並請您離場，且測驗成績不予計分，亦不退費。

# 全民英語能力分級檢定測驗

GENERAL ENGLISH PROFICIENCY TEST

## High-Intermediate Level Speaking Test

**Please read the self-introduction sentence.**

My seat number is (座位號碼後 5 碼) , and my registration number is (考試號碼後 5 碼) .

### Part 1  Answering Questions

You will hear 8 questions. Each question will be spoken once. Please answer the question immediately after you hear it.

For questions 1 to 4, you will have 15 seconds to answer each question.

For questions 5 to 8, you will have 30 seconds to answer each question.

## Part II  Picture Description

Look at the picture, think about the questions below for 30 seconds, and then record your answers for 1½ minutes.

1. Where was this picture taken? What makes you think so?
2. What are the people doing? What kind of people do you think they are?
3. Do your parents or grandparents like this kind of activity? Tell me about their experience.
4. What are the benefits of this activity for elder people? Please explain.
5. If you still have time, please describe the picture in as much detail as you can.

## Part III  Discussion

Think about your answer(s) to the question(s) below for 1½ minutes, and then record your answer(s) for 1½ minutes. You may use your test paper to make notes and organize your ideas.

How is communicating with others online different from interacting with them face-to-face? In what ways do you think Internet usage can improve or undermine our relationship with family and friends? Please explain.

**Please read the self-introduction sentence again.**

My seat number is (座位號碼後 5 碼) , and my registration number is (考試號碼後 5 碼) .

# 複試 寫作測驗 解析

▶▶▶ 第一部分 中譯英 (40%)

將以下這段中文翻譯成英文。

在渴望減重的人當中，有些人寧願嘗試各種藥，而不是改變自己的生活型態。醫師警告，來路不明的減肥藥丸可能極為有害，造成如腎臟損傷之類的副作用。減重最有效的方法是規律的運動和低卡路里飲食。它們相輔相成，其中一個少了另一個就沒有用。少了飲食習慣的改變，多少運動都會是徒勞無功的。

Among those who desire to lose weight, some would rather try various kinds of medications [drugs] instead of changing their own lifestyles. Doctors warn that slimming pills [diet pills / weight-loss pills] from unknown sources could be extremely harmful, causing side effects such as kidney damage. The most effective ways to lose weight are regular exercise and a low-calorie diet. They work hand in hand, and one can't do without the other. Without a change in eating habits, any amount of exercise will be in vain.

逐句說明

## 1. 在渴望減重的人當中，有些人寧願嘗試各種藥，而不是改變自己的生活型態。

Among those who desire to lose weight, some would rather try various kinds of medications [drugs] instead of changing their own lifestyles.

• 「在…當中」：Among...。因為渴望減重的人有很多，所以不能翻譯成

between（在兩者之間）。

- 「…的人」：those who...。those 相當於 those people 的意思。這是很常見的表達方式，一定要記得。同樣的，後面的 some 表示 some of those people 的意思。

- 「寧可做…而不是做…」：would rather do... instead of doing...。請注意 instead of 是介系詞，所以後面接的是動名詞。

- 「各種…」：various kinds of...。也可以翻譯成 different kinds of、all sorts of 或 a variety of。

## 2. 醫師警告，來路不明的減肥藥丸可能極為有害，造成如腎臟損傷之類的副作用。

Doctors warn that slimming pills [diet pills / weight-loss pills] from unknown sources could be extremely harmful, causing side effects such as kidney damage.

- 「來路不明的」：用比較白話的方式來思考，就是 from unknown sources（來自不知道的來源）。或者也可以翻譯成 from unreliable sources（來自不可靠的來源）。

- 這裡把「可能」翻譯成 could 而不是 can，是因為 could 推測的意味比較濃，語氣沒有那麼肯定。不過，用語氣較為肯定的 can 表達醫師的專業意見，其實也是可以的。

- 「副作用」：side effects。

## 3. 減重最有效的方法是規律的運動和低卡路里飲食。

The most effective ways to lose weight are regular exercise and a low-calorie diet.

- 「…的方法」：way to do...。

- 請注意形容詞最高級的後面也有可能接複數名詞，例如這裡「最有效的方法」有兩種，所以應該翻譯成 The most effective ways... are A and B 才對，如果用單數的話就錯了。或者也可以使用另一個類似的表達方式：「Two of the most effective ways to lose weight are...（兩種最有效的減重方法是…）」。

- 這裡是用名詞片語來表達「規律的運動」和「低卡路里飲食」這兩種減

重方式。其實也可以用動名詞片語（doing...）來表達這兩種方法：「Two of the most effective ways to lose weight are exercisng on a regular basis and sticking to a low-calorie diet.（兩種最有效的減重方式是規律運動和堅持低卡路里飲食）」。不過，因為題目的中文翻譯成名詞片語比較直接，翻譯的結果也沒有錯，所以不必刻意改變表達方式寫成動名詞片語。

第1回
第2回
第3回
第4回
第5回
第6回

## 4. 它們相輔相成，其中一個少了另一個就沒有用。

They work hand in hand, and one can't do without the other.

- 這裡把「相輔相成」翻譯成 work hand in hand，意思相當於 work closely together，表示「緊密連結地合作」。

- 「其中一個少了另一個就沒有用」看起來有點繞口，但其實是為了提示翻譯的方法才這樣寫的。兩者的「其中一個」和「另一個」，英文是用 one 和 the other 表達（請注意不要寫成 another〔非特定的另一個〕，在這裡是錯誤的用法，會被扣分）。所以，這部分可以翻譯成 one can't work without the other，但範例翻譯成比較口語的 do without，表示「沒有…也可以（正常運作、達成任務等等）」的意思。

## 5. 少了飲食習慣的改變，多少運動都會是徒勞無功的。

Without a change in eating habits, any amount of exercise will be in vain.

- 「少了…／沒有…」直接用介系詞片語 Without... 來表示，經常用在句子的最前面，修飾整個句子。With... 則是「有了…」或「隨著…」的意思，例如：「With the advance in technology, ...（隨著科技的進步…）」。

- 「徒勞無功」：in vain，也可以當成副詞使用，例如：「They tried to push the whale back into the sea, but in vain.（他們試圖把鯨魚推回海裡，但徒勞無功）」。如果不知道這個表達方式的話，這裡也可以翻譯成 any amount of exercise will not be effective（多少運動都不會有效果）。

依照以下主題，以適當的文體寫一篇 150~180 字的短文。

As artificial intelligence (AI) develops and becomes more common in our daily lives, it is worried that some people, such as translators and accountants, will lose their jobs in the future. However, it is also predicted that the need to cooperate with AI will create new jobs. In your essay, you should
(1) discuss in what ways can AI assist or replace human workers, and
(2) share your thoughts about what will be required to survive in the job market.

隨著人工智慧（AI）發展並且在我們的日常生活中更加常見，有人擔心某些人，例如譯者和會計師，未來將會失去工作。不過，也有人預測和 AI 合作的需求將創造新的工作。在短文中，你應該
(1) 討論 AI 可能在什麼方面協助或取代人類員工，並且
(2) 對於在就業市場上必須具備什麼才能生存，分享你的想法。

**草稿擬定**

根據題目的提示，先設想大致上的文章結構，然後列舉自己想到的細節內容。這些內容可能沒辦法全部寫進文章，但可以作為寫作時的參考。

## 1. AI 可能在什麼方面協助或取代人類員工

→ AI 能做的事：理解說話內容、辨識人臉、翻譯…
what AI can do: understand spoken language, recognize people's faces, translate between languages...

→ 實際運用在企業中的例子：在電話客服中心處理詢問
AI in business: handle inquiries in call centers

→ 對客服中心人員的好處：讓人類有更多時間
benefit for human workers: allow more time for humans

→ 對顧客的好處：減少在電話上等候的時間

benefit for customers: reduce the time of being put on hold

→ 需要的人類員工會比較少 less human workers will be needed

## 2. AI 不具備的人類能力，以及培養這種能力的方法

→ AI 不能做的事：創造性思考、識別人類情緒、有同理心
what AI can't do: think creatively, recognize human emotions, feel empathy

→ AI 不能做的的工作：諮商心理師
a job that AI can't do: counseling psychologist

→ 諮商心理師能做的事：察覺患者的情感、想出個人化的建議
what a counseling psychologist can do: detect a patient's feelings, come up with personalized advices

→ 如何培養這種能力：創意寫作
how to develop such abilities: creative writing

第 1 回　第 2 回　第 3 回　第 4 回　第 5 回　第 6 回

### 重點提示

- 題目給的提示可以作為分段的依據。所以，在第一段可以討論 AI 在企業運用方面取得的成果，第二段則說明人類在工作方面的優越之處。雖然題目沒有明說，但「在就業市場上必須具備的能力」顯然就是 AI 還沒有辦法做到的事。
- 因為篇幅的關係，所以作文範例中沒有深入討論被 AI 取代的人類員工所面臨的困境。如果想要加以討論的話，可以在第二段探討，並且說明政府可以怎樣幫助這些人接受訓練，同時也為還沒進入就業市場的青少年提供課程，讓他們能和新時代的需求接軌，最後再說明需要培養的能力是什麼。
- 題目中提到了譯者和會計師這兩種職業，如果想不到 AI 取代人類的例子，可以從這兩者進行發想。
- 題目中也提示了「和 AI 合作的需求將創造新的工作」，在作文範例中沒有談到，指的主要是人工智慧工程師（AI engineer），他們是負責建立 AI 模型（build AI models）的人。要擔任這項工作，除了寫程式的技術（programming skills）以外，也必須了解統計學（statistics），因為人工智慧的演算法（algorithm）主要是靠統計運作的。

Over the past few years, artificial intelligence (AI) has become an ①integral part of many workplaces. AI can now perform some tasks that we once thought only humans can do, such as understanding spoken language and recognizing people's faces. In ②call centers, for example, speech recognition technology can handle simple inquiries, ③allowing human agents more time to deal with complex problems, and it also reduces the time that customers ④are put on hold. Of course, it also means less human workers will be needed, and many will lose their jobs.

Nevertheless, ⑤it does not seem that AI will eliminate all the job opportunities. AI is incapable of thinking creatively, ⑥not to mention recognizing the depth of human emotions and feelings. Obviously, it is unlikely that jobs which require creative thinking or empathic abilities will be replaced by digital employees. For instance, a counseling psychologist can detect a patient's feelings and ⑦come up with personalized advices, while AI can do nothing like this. To develop such abilities and contend with AI, we can learn to express our thoughts through creative writing, ⑧which inspires our creative mind.

過去幾年,人工智慧(AI)已經成為許多職場不可或缺的一部分。AI 現在能進行我們曾經以為只有人類能做的一些工作,像是理解說話內容,以及辨識人臉。例如在電話客服中心,語音辨識技術能夠處理簡單的詢問,讓人類員工能有更多時間處理複雜的問題,並且也會減少顧客被保留在線上等候的時間。當然,這也意味著需要的人類員工將比較少,而許多人類員工將會失去工作。

儘管如此,AI 看起來並不會消除所有工作機會。AI 不能進行創造性思考,更別說辨識人類情緒和情感的深層了。很明顯,需要創造性思考或同理心(共情)能力的工作不太可能被數位員工取代。舉例來說,諮商心理師能察覺患者的情感,並且想出個人化的建議,而 AI 沒辦法做這樣的事。為了培養這種能力並且和 AI 競爭,我們可以透過激發我們創意思維的創意寫作來學習表達自己的想法。

## 文法分析與替換表達方式

① integral（構成整體所必需的）≒ essential ≒ inseparable

② call center 就是字面上所指的「電話中心」，不管是專門接電話或者是對外打電話，都屬於這一類。如果要細分的話，可以稱呼為提供顧客服務的 customer service center（顧客服務中心）、technical support center（技術支援中心）或者打推銷電話的 telemarketing call center（電話行銷中心）。

③ allowing 是分詞構句，省略了連接詞和主詞，讓整個句子不會因為一直出現同一個主詞（speech recognition technology = it）而顯得呆板單調。從語意上可以推斷分詞構句的部分是表達因果關係，也就是「so it allows...」的意思。

④ be put on hold 是「被保留在電話線上」的意思，雖然和 wait on the line（在電話線上等待）似乎差不多，但被動態更能表達「因為對方無暇處理而被迫等待」的意思。

⑤ it does not seem that...（似乎不…）

　≒ it is unlikely that...（不太可能…）

　≒ it will not be the case that...（情況不會是…）

⑥ not to mention（更不用提…）是用在列舉的時候，強調後者是比前面列舉的事物更理所當然（肯定意味的句子），或者可能性更低（否定意味的句子）。這個句子是列舉 AI 不能（incapable）做的事，所以作者想要表達的是，相較於前面舉出的「創意思考」，後面的「辨識人類情緒和情感的深層」是對 AI 而言難度更高、更不可能做到的事情。not to mention 後面可以接動詞、名詞、形容詞甚至副詞片語。

⑦ come up with（想出）≒ think of ≒ suggest

⑧ 要對前句的受詞進行說明時，經常會選擇使用關係子句（非限定用法），而不是一般的連接詞，因為先行詞和關係子句之間的連結更緊密，容易看出後者說明前者的關係，而能夠避免連接詞後的代名詞有時不太清楚是指什麼的情況。

# 複試 口說測驗 解析

▶▶▶ 第一部分 回答問題

> 你會聽到 8 個問題。每個問題會唸一次。請在聽到題目後立刻回
> 答。第 1 到第 4 題，每題有 15 秒可以回答。第 5 到第 8 題，每題
> 有 30 秒可以回答。

1 **What kind of recreational activity do you do to relieve stress? Why does it help?**
你做什麼休閒活動來紓壓？為什麼這樣有幫助？

答題策略

如果你的休閒活動是運動的話，除了提到你參加的運動，還可以進一步說明
這個運動的好處、你做完運動後的感覺。休閒活動也可以是靜態的活動，例
如下棋（play chess）、看小說（read novels）、聽音樂（listen to music）或
畫畫（paint/draw pictures）。

回答範例 A

Most of the time, I play computer games. Sometimes I play chess or
read novels. These activities help me forget about the stress at work.
Playing computer games is a good form of entertainment.

我大多是玩電腦遊戲。有時候我下棋或讀小說。這些活動能幫我忘掉工作壓力。玩電
腦遊戲是一種很好的娛樂。

回答範例 B

I play badminton with my friends on a regular basis. We meet at least once a week. It helps to keep my body in shape. I always feel refreshed mentally after playing two hours of badminton.

我定期和朋友打羽毛球。我們一週至少見一次面。這能幫助我保持身體健康。打兩個小時的羽毛球之後，我總是覺得心情清爽。

|單字片語| relieve [rɪ`liv] v. 緩和，減輕 / on a regular basis 定期 / in shape 健康的 / refreshed [rɪ`frɛʃt] adj. 恢復了活力的 / mentally [`mɛntl̩ɪ] adv. 心理上，精神上

### 重點補充

關於運動之所以能幫助放鬆的理由，你可以這樣說：

According to a report I read before, exercise helps to release certain chemicals in our brains that help us to relax.（根據我讀過的一份報告，運動有助於釋放大腦中某些幫助我們放鬆的化學物質。）

## 2 Do you enjoy taking selfies? Why or why not?
### 你喜歡自拍嗎？為什麼？

### 答題策略

1. 不管喜不喜歡自拍，照實回答就行了。喜歡自拍的人可以說明自拍的頻率、次數、場地、目的等。不喜歡自拍則可以針對朋友的這種行為提出看法。
2. 你也可以提出自拍時需要注意的事項。例如有些人自拍時跌倒而受傷、有些人自拍時太忘我，結果東西被偷走都不知道。

回答範例 A

I have to admit that I'm kind of addicted to taking selfies. I do it in restaurants, on trains, and even in my bedroom, you name it. I post some of my selfies on Facebook, and I feel great when my friends leave positive comments.

我必須承認自己有點迷自拍。我會在餐廳、列車上、甚至自己臥室自拍，在你想得到的任何地方。我會把一些自拍照 po 到臉書，而朋友留下正面的留言時我覺得很棒。

Selfies? No way. I don't think I'm photogenic. I'm not really fond of taking pictures anyway. I don't understand why some people are always taking selfies as if they are obsessed with themselves.

自拍？不可能，我覺得自己不上相。我終究不太喜歡拍照。我不懂為什麼有些人總是在自拍，好像被自己迷住一樣。

|單字片語| **selfie** [ˋsɛlfɪ] 自拍照 / **be addicted to** 沉迷於… / **you name it** 凡是你想得到的 / **photogenic** [ˌfotəˋdʒɛnɪk] adj. 上相的 / **be fond of** 喜歡…，愛好… / **be obsessed with** 為…著迷

3 **Your cousin Anne has been studying abroad in Australia for a semester. Ask her some questions about her student life.**

你的表妹 Anne 在澳洲留學了一個學期。問她一些關於學生生活的問題。

**答題策略**

1. 關於外國留學的問題很多，你可以問她澳洲跟台灣的學校有什麼不同的地方、那裡的學生是否友善、老師上課的方式為何、課業壓力大不大、有哪些地方不能適應等問題。
2. 因為是近親的關係，你也可以提到比較敏感的話題，例如學費和住宿（tuition and accommodation fees）一個學期要花多少錢？她是否覺得澳洲的男生很帥？

So, how's life in Australia? Did you have a hard time adapting to life in a foreign country? In terms of homework and tests, are schools in

Australia different from those in Taiwan? What about club activities?

所以，在澳洲的生活怎麼樣呢？你適應外國生活有困難嗎？在作業和考試方面，澳洲的學校和台灣不一樣嗎？社團活動呢？

回答範例 B

Tell me about school life over there. Is it very different from Taiwan's? What is your schedule like? Do you have a lot of free time to pursue your hobbies? What are some challenges you face?

跟我説那邊的學校生活。跟台灣很不一樣嗎？你的課程時間表怎麼樣？你有很多空閒時間可以從事自己的嗜好嗎？你遇到什麼樣的困難？

|單字片語| adapt to 適應… / in terms of 在…方面 / schedule [ˋskɛdʒol] n. 時間表；課程表 / pursue one's hobby 從事嗜好活動

4 Your mother is trying to convince your father to quit smoking. Help her persuade your father.
你的母親試圖說服你父親戒菸。幫她說服你的父親。

答題策略

在 15 秒的簡短問答中，最基本的答案往往是最好的答案。你可以簡單列舉兩三個吸菸的害處。或者你也可以從金錢的角度試圖說服爸爸，告訴他抽菸就像在燒錢（is like burning money），一天一包、一年 365 包是很多的錢（one pack a day means 365 packs a year, and they cost a lot of money）。又或者，你可以柔性勸說，告訴爸爸你和媽媽已經吸了很多年的二手菸了（have breathed in secondhand smoke for many years），你不想再這樣了。就算不為自己，爸爸也應該為你們著想（think of...）。

回答範例 A

Dad, you have to realize that there is nothing good about smoking.

Not only does it affect your health badly, but it also makes your teeth yellow. Forgive me for being rude, but I can't stand your bad breath.

爸，你要了解抽菸一點好處也沒有。抽菸不止會嚴重影響你的健康，還會讓你牙齒變黃。恕我無禮，但我真的受不了你的壞口氣。

#### 回答範例 B

Well, Dad. I have to agree with Mom. You've got to quit smoking. Smoking may lead to lung cancer and other diseases. I'm sure you're aware of that. Even the doctor advised you to quit smoking when you did your annual checkup.

嗯，爸。我必須同意媽說的。你一定要戒菸。抽菸可能導致肺癌和其他疾病。我相信你也知道。就連醫生也在你做年度健康檢查的時候建議你戒菸。

|單字片語| there is nothing good about …沒有什麼好的 / forgive me for doing 原諒我做…，恕我… / bad breath 難聞的口氣，口臭 / lung cancer 肺癌 / checkup [ˈtʃɛkˌʌp] n.（身體）檢查

## 5 What do you think are the reasons that many teenagers have mental health problems?
### 你認為許多青少年有心理健康問題的原因是什麼？

### 答題策略

1. 從第 5 題開始，記得要用寫小作文的感覺來回答。也就是說，除了列出可能的答案以外，也要針對每個答案做進一步的說明。如果只是把許多想到的答案列出來，而沒有細節的闡述，是無法獲得高分的。

2. 說到心理問題的原因，我們都會想到壓力（stress），但說明壓力的具體來源才能讓回答顯得充實。常見的壓力來源有學校課業（school work）、父母的期望（expectations from parents）、和朋友的社交關係（social relationships with friends）、參與課外活動（involvement in extracurricular activities）等等。

回答範例 A

Many mental health problems are caused by stress, and for teenagers in Taiwan, I think their stress is mainly related to academic performance. Since our education system places great emphasis on grades, those who don't perform well cannot but feel they're less successful. The situation can get worse when their parents have high expectations and blame them for not getting perfect grades .

許多心理健康問題是由壓力造成的,而對於台灣的青少年來說,我認為他們的壓力主要和學業表現有關。因為我們的教育體系很著重成績,所以表現得不好的人很難不覺得自己比較不成功。當他們的父母有很高的期望,並且責怪他們沒得到完美的成績,情況有可能變得更糟。

回答範例 B

I think teenagers can easily feel hurt in their social lives. When they have difficulty making friends, they may feel isolated and have anxiety about going to school. Even if they are popular at school, they may be persuaded to do things they don't like, such as smoking or drinking, under peer pressure. The stress of fitting in can eventually make them mentally ill.

我認為青少年很容易在社交生活中感覺受傷。當他們在交友方面遇到困難時,他們可能會覺得被孤立,並且對上學感到焦慮。即使他們在學校很受歡迎,也有可能在同儕壓力之下做自己不喜歡的事情,例如抽菸或喝酒。融入環境的壓力,最終可能導致他們產生心理疾病。

|單字片語| **academic performance** 學業表現 / **education system** 教育體系 / **place emphasis on** 強調,著重於… / **peer pressure** 同儕壓力 / **fit in** 融入,和人相處融洽

# Do you think good communication skills are necessary for every kind of job? Please explain.

你認為好的溝通技能對於每種工作都是必要的嗎？請說明。

**答題策略**

1. 擁有好的溝通技能，顯然不是一件壞事，所以選擇肯定的回答，說明溝通技能帶來的好處，應該是比較簡單的答案。不過，因為題目強調 every kind，暗示了少數職業不太需要溝通技能的可能性，所以如果採取否定的回答，以舉例的方式來開頭，並且說明這種職業的人可以靠其他哪些能力取勝，會是比較好的策略。但即使選擇肯定的回答，也應該舉出實際的例子，比較容易獲得高分。

2. 溝通技能為工作帶來的好處，包括幫助解決衝突（help resolve conflicts）、改善生產力（improve productivity）、創造比較良好的關係（create better relationships）、提升專業形象（enhance one's professional image）等等。

**回答範例 A**

Yes, almost all of us need to communicate with our colleagues or clients, and effective communication can facilitate cooperation. For example, we know that software engineers spend a lot of time writing codes, but they still need to communicate with their team members to ensure their codes work right together, and they also need to explain to their clients how their software is meant to function.

是的，我們幾乎所有人都需要和同事或客戶溝通，而有效的溝通能夠促進合作。舉例來說，我們知道軟體工程師花很多時間寫程式碼，但他們還是需要和團隊成員溝通，以確保他們的程式碼放在一起時運作正確，而他們也需要向客戶說明自己的軟體是被設計成怎樣運作的。

第 1 回
第 2 回
第 3 回
第 4 回
第 5 回
第 6 回

回答範例 B

I don't think so. For those who are not good at communicating, there are still plenty of jobs where they can make use of their talents without talking so much. For instance, craftsmen work by themselves, and it's their skills that really matter, so they don't need to be good communicators. Even if they need to promote their works, they can hire someone who is good at public relations.

我不認為。對於不擅長溝通的人,還是有很多他們可以運用自己的才能而不用講那麼多話的工作。舉例來說,工匠是自己工作,真正重要的是他們的技能,所以他們不必是很好的溝通者。就算他們需要宣傳自己的作品,他們也可以雇用擅長公關的人。

|單字片語| facilitate [fəˋsɪləˌtet] v. 使容易,促進 / cooperation [koˌɑpəˋreʃən] n. 合作,協力 / software engineer 軟體工程師 / craftsman [ˋkræftsmən] n. 工匠,工藝師 / public relations 公共關係,公關

## 7

Suppose you are searching for a destination to spend a holiday with your parents. What factors would you consider when deciding on one?

假設你在找和父母度假的目的地。你在選擇的時候會考慮什麼因素?

### 答題策略

因為是跟父母,所以在選擇景點方面要考慮到他們的需求和喜好。除非你的父母不介意坐海盜船和雲霄飛車,不然去遊樂園(amusement park)不太適合。你可以完全從父母的角度下手,把他們喜歡去的國家和喜歡從事的活動說出來。例如你的父親喜歡遊覽城堡和博物館,你的母親喜歡到 outlet 買衣服,你可以選擇一個兩全其美的行程(a plan that is suitable for both of them)。

Well, my parents are not really young anymore. I think distance will be a major consideration. I can't expect them to sit on an airplane for 12 hours. They're not accustomed to eating Western food, so that rules out many countries. Language is also a concern because they can only speak a little English besides Chinese.

嗯，我的父母已經不再年輕了。我想距離會是主要的考量。我不能要求他們坐 12 小時的飛機。他們不習慣吃西餐，所以這排除了很多國家。語言也是我關心的事，因為他們除了中文以外只會說一點英語。

The first thing that comes to my mind is the budget. How much money we're willing to spend on the trip will determine the choice of destination. Another factor I will consider is safety. My mom is very particular about avoiding cities with high crime rates. We want to enjoy the tour and feel safe.

我第一個想到的是預算。我們願意花多少錢，將會決定目的地的選擇。我會考慮的另一個因素是安全。我媽很講究避免高犯罪率的城市這一點。我們想要享受旅行並且感覺安全。

|單字片語| **decide on** 選定… / **consideration** [kənsɪdə`reʃən] n. 考慮的因素 / **be accustomed to** 習慣… / **rule out** 排除…（的可能性） / **concern** [kən`sɝn] n. 關心的事，擔心的事 / **The first thing that comes to my mind is...** 我第一個想到的是… / **be particular about** 對…講究、挑剔 / **crime rate** 犯罪率

# 8 Compared with cram-school education, what are the positive or negative aspects of at-home tutoring?

和補習班教育比起來，家教有什麼優點或缺點？

**答題策略**

1. 即使你沒有請過家教，也可以想像一下。家教肯定比較貴，不過一對一家教（one-on-one tutoring）的效果肯定比一對二十、甚至一對兩百來得好。但話說回來，少了跟同學的互動（interaction with classmates），家教就顯得有點無聊，除非你很喜歡跟自己的家教老師聊天。

2. 如果你或你認識的朋友曾經請過家教，可以說出他們的經驗，好或壞都可以。可能請到的老師很有經驗（was very experienced）、很有愛心（was caring），所以成績突飛猛進（grades improved rapidly）。又或者可能請到不是很好的老師，結果成績還是沒起色（didn't improve）。

**回答範例 A**

Compared with cram-school education, at-home tutoring is more ideal for students with special needs. By special needs, I'm referring to both students who are lagging behind and also those who are way ahead of their peers. Private tutors are able to customize the lessons so that students can learn better. The only negative aspect is the higher cost.

和補習班教育比起來，家教對於有特殊需求的學生比較理想。我說的特殊需求同時指表現落後的學生，和能力超出同儕許多的學生。私人家教能夠量身訂做課程，讓學生可以學得更好。唯一的缺點是費用較高。

**回答範例 B**

I used to have a private tutor. She helped me a lot, and my grades improved within a short time. She clarified many doubts that I had and showed me better ways to memorize new words and understand grammar rules. The only problem we had was changing lesson times to fit her schedule. On the other hand, cram-school education is actually not much different from school education.

我以前有私人家教。她幫了我很大的忙,我的成績也在短時間內進步了。她為我釐清許多疑惑,也教我記新的單字和了解文法規則更好的方式。我們(我跟家教老師)唯一的問題是為了配合她的行程而改變上課時間。另一方面,補習班教育其實跟學校教育沒有很大的不同。

|單字片語| **tutor** [`tjutɚ] n. 家教老師 v. 當家教 / **By..., I'm referring to...** 我說的⋯是指⋯ / **customize** [`kʌstəmˌaɪz] v. 訂做 / **clarify** [`klærəˌfaɪ] v. 澄清,闡明

▶▶▶ 第二部分 看圖敘述

請看照片，用 30 秒的時間思考以下問題，然後用 1 分半的時間錄下你的回答。

1. Where was this picture taken? What makes you think so?
2. What are the people doing? What kind of people do you think they are?
3. Do your parents or grandparents like this kind of activity? Tell me about their experience.
4. What are the benefits of this activity for elder people? Please explain.
5. If you still have time, please describe the picture in as much detail as you can.

1. 這張照片是在哪裡拍的？為什麼你這麼認為？
2. 這些人在做什麼？你認為他們是什麼樣的人？
3. 你的父母或祖父母喜歡這種活動嗎？告訴我他們的經驗。
4. 這項活動對年長者的好處是什麼？請說明。
5. 如果你還有時間，請盡量詳細描述這張照片。

1. 先敘述照片在哪裡拍攝，並舉證說明
2. 提到圖中的人物在做什麼
3. 推測圖中人物的身分
4. 談論長輩的運動習慣，或者不運動、不能運動的原因
5. 討論運動對年長者的好處

老年人運動的好處，除了回答範例中提到的促進身體、心理健康以外，還有預防失智症（dementia）。在談論好處之餘，也可以稍微提到老年人不適合太激烈（strenuous）的運動，或者自己雖然還年輕，但為了在老後保持行動力，所以現在已經養成了運動的習慣，並且會一直持續下去等等。

In the picture, I can see a bench and some large trees on the lawn, so I think this picture was taken in a park. The people are doing outdoor yoga there. There's a female yoga teacher in front of some seniors. I guess they're retired. My parents are much younger than they are. My father and mother are busy earning a living, but my grandparents are about that age. They practice tai chi in a park near their house every morning. I remember doing tai chi with them once, and I felt that deep breathing and slow movements did relieve my stress and anxiety. They told me that doing tai chi reduced their back and knee pain, and they made some new friends in class. I think that's why they look younger and healthier than before. Therefore, I think it's necessary for the elderly to do gentle exercise to stay physically and mentally healthy. Such exercises, like yoga and tai chi, are not strenuous for the elderly, but still help them stay active. It is also said that moderate physical activity helps improve balance and coordination, so it can in turn reduce the risk of falls.

Back to the picture, I see everyone is wearing a short-sleeved

T-shirt, so I guess the photo was taken in summer. From their smiles, I can see they enjoy doing yoga very much.

## 範例中譯

在照片裡，我可以看到一張長凳和草地上的一些大樹，所以我認為這張照片是在公園拍的。人們正在那裡做戶外瑜伽。有一位女性瑜伽老師在一些年長者前面。我猜他們退休了。我爸媽比他們年輕許多。我的爸爸和媽媽忙著賺錢謀生，但我的祖父母差不多是這個年紀。他們每天早上在家附近的公園練習太極拳，我記得跟他們打過一次太極拳，我感覺深呼吸和緩慢的動作的確緩和了我的壓力和焦慮。他們告訴我，打太極拳減少了他們的背痛和膝蓋痛，他們也在課堂上交了一些新朋友。我認為這就是他們看起比以前年輕又健康的原因。所以，我認為老年人必須做和緩的運動來保持身體及心理健康。這種運動，像是瑜伽和太極拳，對於老年人而言不激烈，但仍然能幫助他們保持（身體）活動。據說適度的身體活動也能改善平衡和協調性，也就能減少跌倒的風險。

回到照片，我看見每個人都穿著短袖 T 恤，所以我猜這張照片是在夏天拍的。從他們的笑容，我可以看出他們非常享受做瑜伽。

|單字片語| **retired** [rɪˋtaɪrd] adj. 退休的 / **earn a living** 賺錢謀生 / **tai chi** [ˌtaɪˋtʃi] n. 太極拳 / **strenuous** [ˋstrɛnjʊəs] adj. 費力的，激烈的 / **coordination** [koˌɔrdnˋeʃən] n. 協調

▶▶▶ 第三部分 申述

> 請用 1 分半的時間思考你對於以下問題的答案，然後用 1 分半的時間錄下你的回答。你可以用測驗卷做筆記並整理你的想法。

How is communicating with others online different from interacting with them face-to-face? In what ways do you think Internet usage can improve or undermine our relationship with family and friends? Please explain.

和別人在網路上溝通，與面對面互動有什麼不同？你認為網路的使用會如何促進或傷害我們與家人、朋友的關係？請說明。

1. 網路溝通主要靠文字、表情符號（emoticon [ɪˋmotɪkən] / emoji [ɪˋmodʒɪ]）和貼圖（stickers）。方便、快速，個性害羞的人也可以順利和他人溝通。
2. 面對面溝通需要凝視對方，注意對方的表情（facial expression）和反應。
3. 網路的使用整體來說促進我們與家人、朋友的關係，不過也不能忽略面對面的溝通。

### 回答範例

Due to my personality, I find it hard to talk to people face-to-face. I've always been shy since I was a kid. It feels awkward when someone is looking directly at me. In such situations, I lose my wits and wonder what to say. In fact, I'm so worried about saying the wrong things that I usually just nod or shake my head instead of expressing myself verbally. Strangely, I have no problem whatsoever when I chat with someone online. I can think of a clever response quickly and exercise my sense of humor. The Internet has proven to be indispensable as it helps me stay in touch with my friends and relatives, especially those who live far away. In spite of these advantages, however, I have to admit that there are some hidden risks. People who rely too much on online interaction may have difficulty expressing themselves in front of others. That's exactly the problem I face. During Chinese New Year, my uncles and aunts mentioned that I didn't look them in the eye when I talk to them. When I run out of things to say online, I can always send an emoticon. I don't think that would be a good idea for social gatherings. People exchange comments and compliments spontaneously when they communicate face-to-face. It's a skill that comes only with practice. To sum up, we need to strike a balance between Internet usage and real-life interaction.

### 範例中譯

由於我個性的關係，我覺得很難跟別人面對面交談。我從小就一直很害

羞。有人直視我的時候，感覺很尷尬。在這種情況下，我就會失去冷靜，不知道該說什麼。事實上，我很擔心說錯話，所以通常只是點頭或搖頭，而不是口頭表達自己的想法。奇怪的是，我在網路上和人聊天時就沒有任何問題。我可以很快想到機智的回覆，並且運用我的幽默感。結果證明，（對我而言）網路是不可或缺的，因為它幫助我和朋友、親戚保持聯繫，尤其是那些住得很遠的。不過，雖然有這些優點，我也必須承認（網路）有些隱藏的風險。太過依賴網路互動的人，可能很難在別人面前表達自己的想法。那正是我面對的問題。在農曆新年的時候，叔叔阿姨提到，我跟他們說話時眼睛不直視他們。我在網路上無話可說的時候，我總是可以傳表情符號。我想那在社交聚會上不是個好主意。人們面對面溝通的時候，會自發性地交換意見和稱讚。這是只有靠練習才能得到的技巧。總而言之，我們需要達到網路使用和真實生活互動之間的平衡。

第 1 回 第 2 回 第 3 回 第 4 回 第 5 回 第 6 回

|單字片語| awkward [`ɔkwəd] adj. 令人尷尬的 / lose one's wits 失去理智、冷靜 / express oneself 表達自己的想法；表露自己的感情 / verbally [`vɝbḷɪ] adv. 用語言；口頭上 / no... whatsoever 一點⋯也沒有 / prove to be 結果證明是⋯ / indispensable [ˌɪndɪs`pɛnsəbḷ] adj. 不可或缺的 / stay in touch 保持聯繫 / look someone in the eye 眼睛直視某人 / run out of 用完⋯，耗盡⋯ / emoticon [ɪ`motɪˌkɑn] n. 表情符號 / spontaneously [spɑn`teniəslɪ] adv. 自發地，自然地 / strike a balance between 達成⋯之間的平衡

### 重點補充

關於網路促進關係的部分，你也可以說網路讓你能和分隔兩地的家人、好友聯絡。也可以提到父母（或你本身）在沒有網路的年代傳遞訊息的情況：寫一封信，對方要幾天才能收到，再等對方回信，又是幾天後的事了。

73

# 第三回　寫作能力測驗答題注意事項

1. 本測驗共有兩部分。第一部分為中譯英，第二部分為引導寫作。測驗時間為 **50 分鐘**。

2. 請利用試題紙空白處及背面擬稿，但正答務必書寫在「寫作能力測驗答案紙」上。在答案紙以外的地方作答，不予計分。

3. 第一部分中譯英請在答案紙第一頁開始作答，第二部分引導寫作請自答案紙第二頁起作答。

4. 作答時請勿隔行書寫，請注意字跡應清晰可讀，並請保持答案紙之清潔，以免影響評分。

5. 未獲監試人員指示前，請勿翻閱試卷。

6. 測驗時，不得在考試通知或其他物品上抄題，亦不得有傳遞、夾帶小抄、左顧右盼或交談等違規行為。

7. 意圖或已經將試卷攜出試場者，五年內不得報名參加本測驗。請人代考者，連同代考者，三年內不得報名參加本測驗。

8. 測驗結束時，須立即停止作答，在原位靜候監試人員收回全部試卷及答案紙，清點無誤後，宣佈結束始可離場。

9. 應試者入場、出場及測驗中如有違反上列規則或不服監試人員之指示者，監試人員得取消其應試資格並請其離場，且作答不予計分。

# 全民英語能力分級檢定測驗
## GENERAL ENGLISH PROFICIENCY TEST
## High-Intermediate Level Writing Test

### Part I: Chinese-English Translation (40%)

Translate the following Chinese passage into an English passage, and write your answer on the Writing Test Answer Sheet.

音樂宛如一股神祕的力量，有能力影響我們的心情。它不只能讓我們興奮和喜悅，也能讓我們感動和哀傷。此外，音樂能夠喚起我們的回憶，同時療癒我們的情感創傷。例如，一首歌能夠讓聽者流淚，或者讓他們充滿興奮。音樂是一種沒有邊界或限制的國際通用語言。音樂在你的生命中扮演什麼角色呢？

### Part II: Guided Writing (60%)

Write an essay of **150~180 words** in an appropriate style on the following topic. Write your answer on the Writing Test Answer Sheet.

Due to food safety concerns, some people prefer to eat home-cooked food as much as possible. However, those who simply could not afford the time have no choice but to eat out. Write an essay about your eating habits. In your essay, you should
(1) explain your reasons for eating at home or eating out, and
(2) talk about what a balanced diet should be.

# 全民英語能力檢定測驗

# 中高級寫作能力測驗答案紙

第一部分請由第 1 行開始作答，勿隔行書寫。第二部分請翻至第 2 頁作答。

1 _____

_____

_____

_____

5 _____

_____

_____

_____

10 _____

_____

_____

_____

_____

15 _____

第二部分請翻至第 2 頁作答。

1 _____

_____

_____

_____

5 _____

_____

_____

_____

_____

10 _____

_____

_____

_____

_____

15 _____

_____

_____

_____

_____

20 _____

25

30

35

40

45

50

55

60

# 第三回　口說能力測驗答題注意事項

1. 本測驗問題由耳機播放，回答則經麥克風錄下。分回答問題、看圖敘述與申述題三部份，時間共約 20 分鐘，連同口試說明時間共需約 50 分鐘。

2. 第一部份回答問題的題目只播出一次，聽完題目後請立即回答。第二部份看圖敘述有 30 秒的思考時間及 1 分 30 秒的答題時間；第三部份申述題分別有 1 分 30 秒的思考時間及答題時間。思考時，請不要發出聲音。等聽到指示開始回答時，請針對圖片或申述題的題目在作答時間內盡量的表達。

3. 錄音設備皆已事先完成設定，請勿觸動任何機件，以免影響錄音。測驗時請戴妥耳機，將麥克風調到嘴邊約三公分處，依指示以適中音量回答。

4. 測驗進行間，不可以在試題紙以外任何物品上書寫與測驗相關之任何文字、符號，亦不可有傳遞、夾帶小抄、左顧右盼或交談等違規行為，否則作答不予計分。

5. 意圖或已將試題紙或試題影音資料攜出或傳送出試場者，視同侵犯本中心著作財產權，限五年內不得報名參加「全民英檢」測驗。請人代考者，連同代考者，三年內不得報名參加本測驗。

6. 測驗結束時，須立即停止作答，在原位靜候監試人員收回全部試題紙並清點無誤，等候監試人員宣布結束後始可離場。

7. 入場、出場及測驗中如有違反上列規則或不服監試人員之指示者，監試人員將取消您的應試資格並請您離場，且測驗成績不予計分，亦不退費。

# 全民英語能力分級檢定測驗
## GENERAL ENGLISH PROFICIENCY TEST
## High-Intermediate Level Speaking Test

**Please read the self-introduction sentence.**

My seat number is (座位號碼後 5 碼) , and my registration number is (考試號碼後 5 碼) .

## Part 1　Answering Questions

You will hear 8 questions. Each question will be spoken once. Please answer the question immediately after you hear it.

For questions 1 to 4, you will have 15 seconds to answer each question.

For questions 5 to 8, you will have 30 seconds to answer each question.

## Part II  Picture Description

Look at the picture, think about the questions below for 30 seconds, and then record your answers for 1½ minutes.

1. Where was this picture probably taken? What makes you think so?
2. What are the group of people in the center doing? Have you ever seen such a scene in person? Tell me about your experience.
3. What are on the left and right sides of the picture? What might people do there?
4. Do you enjoy occasions like this? Please explain.
5. If you still have time, please describe the picture in as much detail as you can.

## Part III  Discussion

Think about your answer(s) to the question(s) below for 1½ minutes, and then record your answer(s) for 1½ minutes. You may use your test paper to make notes and organize your ideas.

Have you tried watching movies via a streaming service? How is it different from going to a theater? Do you think movie theaters will still exist in the future? Please explain.

**Please read the self-introduction sentence again.**

My seat number is (座位號碼後 5 碼) , and my registration number is (考試號碼後 5 碼) .

第 3 回

第 1 回
第 2 回
第 3 回
第 4 回
第 5 回
第 6 回

# 複試 寫作測驗 解析

▶▶▶ 第一部分 **中譯英** (40%)

將以下這段中文翻譯成英文。

音樂宛如一股神祕的力量，有能力影響我們的心情。它不只能讓我們興奮和喜悅，也能讓我們感動和哀傷。此外，音樂能夠喚起我們的回憶，同時療癒我們的情感創傷。例如，一首歌能夠讓聽者流淚，或者讓他們充滿興奮。音樂是一種沒有邊界或限制的國際通用語言。音樂在你的生命中扮演什麼角色呢？

**翻譯範例**

Music is like a mysterious force, which has the power to affect our mood. It can not only make us excited and joyful, but it can also make us touched and sorrowful. In addition, music can arouse our memories and heal our emotional wounds at the same time. For example, a song can bring listeners to tears or fill them with excitement. Music is a universal language that has no boundaries or limits. What role does music play in your life?

**逐句說明**

**1. 音樂宛如一股神祕的力量，有能力影響我們的心情。**

Music is like a mysterious force, which has the power to affect our mood.

• 「宛如…」：be like...。雖然中文看起來有點難，但理解成「像是…」就不難了。其他表示「很像」或「類似」的表達方式有：seem like（看起來像…）、be akin to（和…相似）、can be compared to（可以比作…）。不過，這裡還是最簡單的 be like 最符合題意。

- 「影響」：affect（動詞）。注意不要寫成 effect（名詞）。雖然 effect 也有動詞的用法，但當動詞時表示「實現」或「達到」的意思。除了 affect 以外，也可以用 influence（動、名詞同形）表示「影響…」。impact（動、名詞同形）雖然也有「影響」的意思，但在這裡比較不適合，因為它具有「像衝擊一般帶來強烈影響（經常是負面的）」的含義。

## 2. 它不只能讓我們興奮和喜悅，也能讓我們感動和哀傷。

It can not only make us excited and joyful, but it can also make us touched and sorrowful.

- 這裡看起來有很多內容，但只要掌握主要的結構就沒那麼難。句型是「它不只能…也能…」，所以英文的結構是「It can not only..., but it can also...」。因為兩邊的句子有重複的內容，所以後半可以省略成「but (also) make us touched and sorrowful」。再極端一點，甚至可以省略成「but also touched and sorrowful」。另外，對於母語人士來說，其實把 not only 移到句首會是比較自然的說法，這時候第一個子句的助動詞會移到主詞前面，如下：「Not only can it make us excited and joyful, but it can also...」。

- 這裡的形容詞不一定要照著範例來翻譯，但之所以選擇這些單字，是因為字尾相同（excited－touched、joyful－sorrowful），有對仗的效果。

## 3. 此外，音樂能夠喚起我們的回憶，同時療癒我們的情感創傷。

In addition, music can arouse our memories and heal our emotional wounds at the same time.

- 「此外」：In addition。這裡也可以翻譯成 Besides、What's more、On top of that。

- 「喚起回憶」：arouse memories。動詞也可以換成 evoke（喚起）或 revive（使復活）。

- 「療癒創傷」：heal wounds。

4. 例如，一首歌能夠讓聽者流淚，或者讓他們充滿興奮。

**For example, a song can bring listeners to tears or fill them with excitement.**

- 「讓聽者流淚」：bring/move listeners to tears。如果不知道這個說法的話，就翻譯成 make listeners cry，雖然沒有那麼文雅，但至少比放棄不寫來得好。

5. 音樂是一種沒有邊界或限制的國際通用語言。

**Music is a universal language that has no boundaries or limits.**

- 「國際通用語言」：a universal language。universal 表示「普遍通用的」，例如 love is universal（愛是普遍存在而通行無阻的）。這裡也可以翻譯成 an internationally-accepted language（國際上接受的語言）、a globally-recognized language（全球認同的語言）。
- 「邊界」：boundaries。雖然 border 也是「邊界」的意思，但通常是指國界之類具體的界線，而 boundary 則可以指具體或抽象的界線，例如影響力或能力所及的範圍，所以這裡的翻譯選擇了 boundary。

6. 音樂在你的生命中扮演什麼角色呢？

**What role does music play in your life?**

- 「扮演角色」：play a role。

▶▶▶ 第二部分 引導寫作 (60%)

依照以下主題，以適當的文體寫一篇 150~180 字的短文。

Due to food safety concerns, some people prefer to eat home-cooked food as much as possible. However, those who simply could not afford the time have no choice but to eat out. Write an essay about your eating habits. In your essay, you should

第 1 回
第 2 回
第 3 回
第 4 回
第 5 回
第 6 回

(1) explain your reasons for eating at home or eating out, and
(2) talk about what a balanced diet should be.

由於食品安全的顧慮，有些人偏好盡量多吃在家烹調的食物。然而，沒時間做菜的人除了外食以外別無選擇。請寫一篇關於你飲食習慣的短文。在短文中，你應該
(1) 說明你在家吃飯或外食的理由，並且
(2) 談論均衡的飲食應當如何。

**草稿擬定**

根據題目的提示，先設想大致上的文章結構，然後列舉自己想到的細節內容。這些內容可能沒辦法全部寫進文章，但可以作為寫作時的參考。

## a. 在家吃飯的理由

→ 健康、安全得多 much healthier and safer

→ 可以選擇新鮮的食材 can select fresh ingredients

→ 避開人潮 avoid the crowd

→ 不需要等待 no need to wait

→ 在家比較舒服 more comfortable at home

→ 比在高級餐廳用餐便宜
 less expensive compared with dining in fine restaurants

→ 享受烹飪的樂趣 enjoy the fun of cooking

## b. 外食的理由

→ 省時、省麻煩 save time; trouble-free

→ 比較省錢 cheaper / can save money

→ 比較多選擇和種類 more choices and variety

→ 比較美味、吸引人 more delicious and appealing

**重點提示**

・對於二選一的題目，有時候符合你實際情況的選擇，可能反而是比較不容易發揮的答案。所以選擇答案時，最好考慮對你來說好不好寫。在上面草

稿擬定的階段，試著對於兩個選擇都列出一些理由，發現「在家吃飯」想到的理由比較多，表示這個答案對我來說可能是比較容易發揮的，所以例文就以在家吃飯比較安全、健康作為主要論點。當然情況也有可能相反，這時候就應該選擇另一個答案。

- 在寫作的時候，通常寫自己的經驗比較好，因為比較熟悉，內容也會比較充實。如果自己沒有相關的經驗，也可以從身邊的親朋好友尋找題材。在例文中，因為自己沒什麼做菜的經驗，主要是媽媽下廚，所以就用她做菜的習慣作為文章的主要內容。

- 除了題目最後要求必須寫出來的事項以外，其實前面的文字敘述也是很重要的提示。例如這裡的題目就已經提到食安問題（在家吃飯的理由）、沒有時間（外食的理由）這兩點，所以例文選擇先談論食安問題，並且舉出黑心食品的案例，進而導向媽媽堅持自己做飯這一點，還有自己選擇食材、避免吃進有害化學物質等好處。

- 第二段要談論什麼才是均衡的飲食。我們大多會想到少吃垃圾食物、多吃蔬菜水果等原則，但除此之外，也要具體舉一些例子，內容才充實。如果覺得自己平常的飲食習慣還算健康，可以直接描述自己三餐的內容。

## 作文範例

①Sad as it may be, ②it is no longer a surprise to read about "food scandals". Recently, a well-established food manufacturer ③was found using ingredients that ④had expired for three years. ⑤In view of these food safety concerns, my mother ⑥insists that we eat home-cooked meals every day, except on special occasions like birthdays or anniversaries. ⑦By choosing the ingredients we use, we can reduce the risk of taking in chemicals that are harmful to health.

Besides being careful about ingredients, we also need to maintain a balanced diet to stay healthy. Fortunately, my mother is also good at ⑧the latter. Our family breakfast ⑨consists of hard-boiled eggs, an assortment of nuts, two types of fruits dependent on the season of the year, and pieces of toast spread with organic chocolate or peanut butter. For dinner, we usually have moderate ⑩amounts of meat and fresh salad. Junk food such as French fries, fried chicken, and pizzas never appear on our family menu. By simply eating at home, I have learned how to eat well.

範例中譯

　　雖然可能很悲哀，但現在讀到關於黑心食品的消息（「食物醜聞」）已經不是件意外的事。最近有一家有信譽的食品製造業者被發現使用過期三年的原料。考慮到這些食品安全顧慮，我的母親堅持我們要每天吃家裡做的餐點，除了生日或週年紀念日之類的特殊場合以外。藉著選擇我們使用的食材，我們能減少攝取到有害健康的化學物質的風險。

　　除了小心注意食材以外，我們也必須維持均衡的飲食以維持健康。幸運的是，我的母親也很擅長後者。我們家的早餐包含水煮蛋、綜合堅果、兩種依時令決定的水果，還有幾片塗上有機巧克力醬或花生醬的烤吐司。至於晚餐，我們通常吃適量的肉和新鮮沙拉。薯條、炸雞、披薩之類的垃圾食物從來不會出現在我們家的菜單上。只靠著在家吃飯，我就學到了該怎麼吃得健康。

文法分析與替換表達方式

① (as) sad as it may be, ...（雖然可能很悲哀，但…）。這個開頭的方式是表達寫文章的人對這個負面情況的態度。也可以說 It is sad to say (so), but...（雖然說起來很悲哀，但…），但注意後面這個說法要加 but。

② it is no longer a surprise to read about "food scandals"
讀到關於黑心食品的消息已經不是件意外的事
≒ we no longer find it a surprise when we read about "food scandals"
讀到關於黑心食品的消息時，我們不再感覺驚訝

③ 雖然也可以用主動態 The authorities found（相關當局發現…），但因為這裡的重點是黑心食品廠商，誰發現的不是很重要，所以用被動態 a food manufacturer was found 省略不提發現者是誰。

④ 過去某個時間發現這件事的時候，原料已經過期了，所以用過去完成式 had expired 表達，而不是用現在完成式 have expired。

⑤ In view of...（考慮到…）。字面上的意思是「在看到…的情況下」，表示考慮某個事實之後，據此採取接下來的行動或想法，也可以翻譯成「鑑於…」。雖然這裡也可以使用 Because of、Due to、As a result of 這些表示「因為、由於」的說法，但它們表達的是直接的因果關係，原因所產生的結果有一定的必然性；In view of 則是表示考慮某件事之後採取行動或產生想法，實際上可能並不是非這麼做不可，是因為行為者本身的判斷或偏好才如此。

⑥ 請注意表示「建議、要求」（例如 insist、demand、suggest 等等）的動詞後面接子句時，子句中的動詞會使用原形動詞或 should do 的形態，例如：「She insisted that he (should) apologize to her.（她堅持要他道歉）」。

⑦ By doing...（藉由做…）。要表示某個行為是做到另一件事的方法時，這是很好用的表達方式。

⑧ 因為前面提到了 being careful about ingredients 和 maintain a balanced diet 兩件事，所以如果只說 my mother is also good at "it" 的話，會讓人搞不清楚是指哪件事。當文章前面提到了兩個人或事物，後面要再次提到這兩者或其中之一的時候，會使用 the former（前者）和 the latter（後者）的說法。所以，這裡用 the latter 是表示 my mother is also good at maintaining a balanced diet。

⑨ consist of... 由…組成
  ≒ be comprised of...
  ≒ be made up of...
  ≒ include...（包括…）
  ≒ contain...（含有…）

⑩ an amount of...（某個量的…）後面接不可數名詞，a number of...（一些…）後面接可數名詞。amount/number 前面可以用 large、small、moderate（適中的）等形容詞修飾。amount、number 本身都是可數名詞，例文中使用複數的 amounts of meat and fresh salad 來表達，是因為吃晚餐的次數很多，複數的 amounts 隱含「每次晚餐的內容各有不同」的意義。

# 複試 口說測驗 解析

你會聽到 8 個問題。每個問題會唸一次。請在聽到題目後立刻回答。第 1 到第 4 題,每題有 15 秒可以回答。第 5 到第 8 題,每題有 30 秒可以回答。

## 1 Have you ever witnessed a traffic accident? Tell me about your experience.

你目擊過車禍嗎?告訴我你的經驗。

**答題策略**

大多數人應該曾經路過發生車禍的地方,但不一定目睹過車禍發生的瞬間。你可以說自己在車禍發生後路過的經驗,敘述你看到的情形。除此之外,也可以引述其他目擊者的話,或者談一下交通安全的重要性。

**回答範例 A**

A few weeks ago, I saw a traffic accident on the freeway. A car collided with a truck. It was a horrible sight. I wondered if the driver survived the accident. I told myself to be extra careful when driving.

幾個禮拜前,我在高速公路上看到了車禍。一台汽車和卡車撞在一起。那是很可怕的景象。我疑惑駕駛在車禍後有沒有活下來。我告訴自己開車時要格外小心。

**回答範例 B**

I've never seen a traffic accident in person, only on TV. I think if we follow traffic rules and have a little more patience, many accidents can be avoided.

我沒有親眼看過車禍，只在電視上看過。我想如果我們遵守交通規則，並且有多一點耐心的話，很多意外是可以避免的。

|單字片語| witness [`wɪtnɪs] v. 目擊 / freeway [`fri͵we] n. （美）高速公路 / collide [kə`laɪd] v. 碰撞 / in person 親身，親自

### 重點補充

在美國，除了 freeway 以外，也有些地區習慣把高速公路稱為 expressway。據說台灣最初興建高速公路時聘請了美國加州的顧問，所以使用當地習慣的「freeway」作為高速公路的名稱。freeway 的 free 並不是「免費」的意思，應該理解為「沒有紅綠燈」比較恰當。日本、中國大陸則使用 expressway 作為譯名。一般的公路都可以稱為 highway。另外，英國的高速公路稱為 motorway。

## 2　Do you get along well with your neighbors? Why or why not?
你跟鄰居相處融洽嗎？為什麼？

### 答題策略

你可能很少看到鄰居，不過你可以說媽媽或奶奶跟他們的互動情形。如果真的完全不知道鄰居是誰，也可以據實回答，並且說明理由，例如鄰居長時間在美國（live in the US most of the time），或者大家出門和回家的時間不一樣（leave and go home at different times）。

#### 回答範例 A

I get along pretty well with my neighbors. They're very friendly and helpful. In fact, we're like good friends. We exchange gifts and food during festivals.

我跟鄰居相處得蠻好的。他們很友善，也很幫忙。事實上，我們就像好朋友一樣。我們在節慶時會交換禮物和食物。

Not really. We seldom talk to one another, even when we meet in an elevator. Some of my neighbors like to leave their things outside their apartments. My parents tried to talk to them, but it didn't work.

不太好。我們彼此很少說話,就算在電梯裡見到也是。有些鄰居喜歡把東西放在自家（公寓）門外。我爸媽試圖跟他們談,但沒有用。

|單字片語| **get along with** 與…和睦相處

### 重點補充

雖然英文沒有簡單表示「遠親不如近鄰」的成語,不過還是可以解釋一下。

As a Chinese saying goes, your next-door neighbors are more important than relatives living far away. I think it is very true, especially in the event of an emergency.（就像中文的格言說的,你的隔壁鄰居比住在遠處的親戚更重要。我想這非常對,尤其是在萬一發生緊急情況的時候。）

## 3 Your cousin Adam just married his long-time partner. Ask him some questions about his life after marriage.

你的表哥 Adam 剛和交往已久的對象結婚。問他一些關於婚後生活的問題。

### 答題策略

1. 注意題目要求的問題是「婚後生活」,所以如果問對方的交往過程、決定結婚的理由之類的,就不符合題意了。因為已經過了戀愛而進入共同生活的階段,所以可以問一些比較實際的問題,例如是否共同分擔家事（share the housework）、是否和父母同住（live with your parents）、妻子是否和父母相處融洽（get along with your parents）等等。
2. 如果只是丟出一連串的問題,可能會感覺不太自然,所以可以在開頭先恭喜對方,或者稱讚對方的妻子之類的,再開始問問題。

第 1 回
第 2 回
第 3 回
第 4 回
第 5 回
第 6 回

回答範例 A

Congratulations on your new life. Now that you live with your wife, do you see different sides of her? And how do you settle disagreements about chores and responsibilities?

恭喜你有了新的生活。既然你現在和老婆一起生活，你有看到她不同的面貌嗎？還有你們是怎麼解決家事和責任方面的爭吵？

回答範例 B

Wow! You look better after marriage. I know that you still live with your parents, so does your wife get along with them? Are you planning to buy a home and move out in the future?

哇！你結婚後看起來更好了。我知道你還和父母住在一起，所以你的老婆跟他們相處融洽嗎？你們未來打算買房子並且搬出去嗎？

|單字片語| **disagreement** [ˌdɪsəˋgrimənt] **n.** 意見不合，爭吵

4   **Your friend Lisa is considering opening a coffee shop, but she lacks experience. Give her some advice.**

**你的朋友 Lisa 正在考慮開咖啡店，但她缺乏經驗。給她一些建議。**

**答題策略**

1. 有兩個方向，一個是支持她的決定，並且建議如何彌補經驗不足的問題；另一個是勸阻她，希望她不要在經驗不足的情況下貿然行動。不管是哪種回答，都應該談到「經驗不足」這方面，才算是完整的回答。
2. 你也可以製造一些虛構的劇情，例如你的朋友正好有一家咖啡店，她可以在那裡打工（do a part-time job）來學習經營咖啡店的基礎（basics of running a coffee shop）。

While people today drink a lot of coffee, the coffee shop industry is quite competitive. Since you have no experience running a coffee shop, you'd better buy a franchise. It would be much easier.

雖然現在的人喝很多咖啡，但咖啡店行業很競爭。因為你沒有經營咖啡店的經驗，所以你最好加盟連鎖。那樣會簡單很多。

回答範例 B

I know you are passionate about opening a coffee shop, but that's not enough. You should be familiar with the business. More importantly, you need a clear and solid business plan.

我知道你對於開咖啡店充滿熱情，但那還不夠。你應該熟悉這項事業。更重要的是，你需要清楚而穩健的商業計畫。

|單字片語| **buy a franchise** 購買特許經銷權（也就是加盟連鎖業者的意思）/ **be passionate about** 對於⋯有熱情 / **business plan** 商業計畫

## 5  What can everyone do in their everyday life to help fight global warming?
### 每個人可以在日常生活中做什麼來幫助對抗全球暖化？

**答題策略**

1. 從第五題開始，作答時間為 30 秒，通常會問一些發揮空間比較多的話題。在日常生活中，我們可以透過節能減碳（save energy and reduce carbon emission）來保護地球。可以稍微說明全球暖化的原因，再提出解決的方法，但因為題目的重點還是在於日常生活中具體的行動，所以不要花太多時間說明原因，以免沒時間講關於具體行動的部分。

2. 保護環境有所謂的「3R」：reduce、reuse、recycle，如果好好發揮，其實說明其中一個就能撐過 30 秒。例如減少的部分，除了減少垃圾，也可以提到減少使用塑膠袋（reduce the use of plastic bags）、減少用電（reduce the use of electricity），並且舉例說明。

回答範例 A

Global warming is a growing concern indeed. We may not be scientists or politicians, but we can still do our part to save the Earth. For example, take public transportation instead of driving. Cars are one of the main causes of air pollution that leads to global warming. Conserving power is also a way to help fight global warming.

全球暖化的確是越來越令人擔憂的事。我們或許不是科學家或政治人物，但我們還是可以盡一己之力保護地球。例如，搭乘大眾運輸工具而不要開車。汽車是導致全球暖化的空氣污染的主要來源之一。節省電力也是一個幫助對抗全球暖化的方法。

回答範例 B

One of the causes of global warming is the burning of trash. As individuals, we can reduce the amount of garbage we produce by recycling things like plastic bottles, metal cans, and papers. I ride a bike to school rather than ride a scooter because scooters are also responsible for global warming.

全球暖化的原因之一是焚燒垃圾。身為個人，我們可以藉由回收塑膠瓶、金屬罐和紙張之類的東西來減少我們產生的垃圾量。我騎單車上學而不是騎機車，因為機車也是造成全球暖化的原因。

|單字片語| **global warming** 全球暖化 / **concern** [kən`sɝn] n. 擔心，關心的事 / **do one's part** 做好份內的事，盡一己之力 / **conserve** [kən`sɝv] v. 保存，節省 / **scooter** [`skutɚ] n. 輕型機車（這個字也常指「滑板車」，要明確指機車時，可以說 **motor scooter**）

# What do you think are some qualities and traits that successful inventors have in common?

你認為成功的發明家共同的特質是什麼？

**答題策略**

1. 關鍵字為成功的 inventors（發明家），發明家在成功之前肯定需要經歷許多失敗（fail many times）。永不放棄（never give up）是許多發明家共同的特質。此外，他們也需要有創意（be creative）、聽別人的意見（listen to other people's opinions）、從自己的錯誤中學習（learn from their mistakes）。

2. 平時閱讀一些知名人物的故事，像是藝術家、作家、音樂家、商人、政治人物等，遇到適當的題目時就能夠發揮。

回答範例 A

This is a tough one. A successful inventor has to be able to overcome many obstacles without losing their passion. They may fail again and again before they come up with a successful invention. They must learn from their mistakes and look for better solutions to the problems they face. In short, they have to be persistent.

這是很難的問題。成功的發明家必須能夠克服許多障礙而不失去熱情。在想出成功的發明之前，他們可能會一再失敗。他們必須從錯誤中學習，並且為他們面臨的問題尋找更好的解決方法。簡而言之，他們必須堅持不懈。

回答範例 B

Thomas Edison was one of the world's most successful inventors. He pointed out that genius is one percent inspiration and 99 percent perspiration. Before he invented the light bulb, he failed many times. He viewed each failure as a learning experience. I think hard work, discipline, and determination are necessary for an inventor to be successful.

湯瑪士‧愛迪生是世界上最成功的發明家之一。他指出，天才是百分之 1 的靈感和百分之 99 的汗水。在他發明燈泡之前，他失敗了許多次。他把每次失敗看成學習的經驗。我認為發明家要成功，努力、紀律和決心是必要的。

|單字片語| **trait** [tret] n. 特徵，特點 / **inventor** [ɪnˋvɛntə] n. 發明者，發明家 / **obstacle** [ˋɑbstək!] n. 障礙 / **come up with** 想出⋯ / **persistent** [pəˋsɪstənt] adj. 堅持不懈的 / **inspiration** [ˌɪnspəˋreʃən] n. 靈感 / **perspiration** [ˌpɝspəˋreʃən] n. 汗，流汗 / **light bulb** 燈泡 / **discipline** [ˋdɪsəplɪn] n. 紀律 / **determination** [dɪˌtɝməˋneʃən] n. 決心

## 7　What are the pros and cons of renting a car while traveling in a foreign country?

### 在外國旅行時租車的優缺點是什麼？

**答題策略**

就算沒有租車的經驗，也要硬著頭皮作答。因為是在國外，所以不是比較購車和租車的選擇，而是租車和搭乘公共運輸的利與弊。

回答範例 A

The most obvious advantage is the time we save. Waiting for trains and buses can take away the precious time we have for a trip. With a rented car, we have the freedom to go to places without bus stops or train stations. What's more, we can stop anywhere and anytime we want to take a picture. One problem would be the high cost of renting a car.

最明顯的優點是我們節省的時間。等待列車和巴士會奪走我們旅行的寶貴時間。有了租來的車，我們就能夠自由前往沒有公車站或火車站的地方。而且，我們可以隨時隨地停下來照相。一個問題會是租車的高額費用。

回答範例 B

Renting a car while traveling in a foreign country is definitely a good way to explore new places. It could be cheaper than taking trains, especially in European countries. It's also much more convenient. However, it can be dangerous if we are not familiar with the area. Getting lost in a foreign country sounds frightening.

在外國旅行時租車絕對是探索新地點的好方法。這樣可能會比搭列車便宜，尤其在歐洲國家。這樣也便利得多。不過，如果我們對那個區域不熟悉的話，可能會有危險。在外國迷路聽起來很可怕。

|單字片語| **pros and cons** 贊成和反對的理由；優點和缺點 / **what's more** 而且，更有甚者（繼續列舉支持論述的理由時使用的插入語）

## 8 Do you agree that envy can motivate us to improve ourselves? Please explain.
你同意羨慕能夠刺激我們改進自己嗎？請說明。

**答題策略**

羨慕跟嫉妒只有一線之隔，羨慕別人表示我們也想跟他們一樣，想要過他們的生活。把別人當作自己未來的目標，的確有助於讓自己更有動力。不過，羨慕也可能讓我們失去自信。如果能夠同時說明羨慕帶來的正面和負面效果，會是比較完整的答案。

回答範例 A

I believe it works for some people, including me. When we envy someone, we want to have the wonderful things they have in life, such as a nice car, a bigger home, or a better job. To achieve that, we have to work hard to improve ourselves. Therefore, envy can be a powerful form of motivation. Nevertheless, envy shouldn't be turned into jealousy.

我相信這對一些人有用，包括我。當我們羨慕別人的時候，我們會想要他們在生活中擁有的美好事物，像是很好的車、更大的房子或更好的工作。為了達到目標，我們必

須努力改進自己。所以，羨慕可以是一種有力的動機。儘管如此，也不應該把羨慕變成嫉妒。

回答範例 B

I agree to a certain extent. When I'm envious of my friends' grades, I work harder so that I can get better grades. It's a negative emotion, but it motivates me to improve myself. However, sometimes it can backfire. Envy can make you lose confidence in yourself. You start to believe that you can never be as good and there is no point trying.

我在某種程度上同意。當我羨慕朋友的成績時，我就會更努力，以求獲得更好的成績。這是一種負面情緒，但可以刺激我改善自己。不過，有時候羨慕也會產生反效果。羨慕可能使你失去自信。你會開始相信自己永遠不會變得一樣好，而努力是沒有意義的。

│單字片語│ **motivate** [`motə͵vet] v. 刺激，給予動機 / **motivation** [͵motə`veʃən] n. 刺激，動機 / **to a certain extent** 到一定的程度；在某種程度上 / **backfire** [`bæk`faɪr] v. 產生反效果 / **There is no point doing** 做⋯沒有意義

### 重點補充

前面提過某個非特定的單數人物，例如 someone、a person 之後，要用代名詞指稱時，正統的做法是以「he or she」指稱，但近代不論口語或書面語，有越來越多人會用複數「they」來指稱，就像回答範例 A 一樣：「When we envy someone, we want to have the wonderful things they have in life...」。因為可以避免代名詞的性別問題，所以這已經成為許多人接受的說法。

> 請看照片,用 30 秒的時間思考以下問題,然後用 1 分半的時間錄下你的回答。

1. Where was this picture probably taken? What makes you think so?
2. What are the group of people in the center doing? Have you ever seen such a scene in person? Tell me about your experience.
3. What are on the left and right sides of the picture? What might people do there?
4. Do you enjoy occasions like this? Please explain.
5. If you still have time, please describe the picture in as much detail as you can.

1. 這張照片可能是在哪裡拍的?為什麼你這麼認為?
2. 照片中間那群人在做什麼?你親眼看過這個景象嗎?告訴我你的經驗。
3. 照片左右兩邊有什麼?人們可能在那裡做什麼?
4. 你喜歡像這樣的場合嗎?請說明。
5. 如果你還有時間,請盡量詳細描述這張照片。

**草稿擬定**

1. 說明圖中的天氣並發表意見
2. 描述中間身穿制服的軍樂隊
3. 提及左下方的婦女和兩個孩子
4. 猜測圖中人物的心情
5. 對於類似的活動提出看法

**加分延伸**

你可以補充說，藉由參加這類節慶活動（festival），有可能認識並體驗不同國家的文化、習俗和美食（culture, customs, and cuisines of different countries）。

**回答範例**

This picture was taken outdoors on a bright and sunny day. The weather is perfect for a family outing. I see a woman with two children at the left bottom of the picture. The woman is wearing a hat, and so is the man on the right. I guess it must be pretty warm. The man, woman, and children are all attracted to a group of people in uniform. They resemble British soldiers with the unique hats they are wearing. With their backs to me, I can't tell if they are foreigners from England or Taiwanese dressed up as British soldiers. The last soldier is carrying a large drum. Everyone has their eyes glued to the military band. Though I can't hear them play, I can visualize the uplifting music and festive atmosphere. It seems like there is a carnival going on. There are many canopies on either side of the band. On the right, vendors set up stands to sell probably their local products or handicrafts. It's a pity that I can't see what they have on display because the items are too small. On the left side of the band, there's a larger canopy with foldable tables and chairs. I think it's an area set aside for people to eat their meals. It's a nice touch because after walking around, visitors may feel tired and hungry.

I enjoy community events like the one shown in the picture. I'm particularly interested in the stalls. I usually purchase some handicrafts as souvenirs.

範例中譯

這張照片是在晴朗日子的戶外拍攝的。天氣非常適合家庭出遊。我看到左下角有一名女子帶著兩個小孩。這位女子戴著帽子，右邊的男子也是。我猜天氣一定很暖和。男子、女子和小孩都被一群穿制服的人吸引了。他們戴著獨特的帽子，看起來像英國士兵。因為他們背對著我，所以我看不出來他們是來自英國的外國人，還是裝扮像英國士兵的台灣人。最後面的士兵背著大鼓。每個人的眼睛都注視著這支軍樂隊。雖然我聽不到他們演奏，但我可以想像振奮人心的音樂和節慶的氣氛。那裡看起來像在進行嘉年華會。樂隊的兩邊有很多棚子。在右邊，攤販設置了攤位，可能是賣當地產品或手工藝品。可惜我看不到他們展示什麼，因為東西太小了。樂隊左邊有比較大的棚子，有摺疊桌和摺疊椅。我想這是設在旁邊讓人用餐的區域。這能為活動增色，因為到處走動之後，遊客可能會覺得又累又餓。我很喜歡照片中顯示的這種社區活動。我對攤位特別有興趣。我通常會買一些手工藝品當紀念。

|單字片語| **outing** [ˋaʊtɪŋ] n. 短途的出遊 / **in uniform** 穿著制服的 / **resemble** [rɪˋzɛmbl̩] v. 像，類似… / **dress up** 裝扮 / **have one's eyes glued to** 眼睛緊盯著… / **visualize** [ˋvɪʒʊəˌlaɪz] v. 想像（看到…的形影、畫面）/ **uplifting** [ʌpˋlɪftɪŋ] adj. 振奮人心的 / **festive** [ˋfɛstɪv] adj. 節慶的 / **carnival** [ˋkɑrnəvl̩] n. 嘉年華會 / **canopy** [ˋkænəpɪ] n. 棚子 / **vendor** [ˋvɛndɚ] n. 小販 / **stand** [stænd] n. 攤子 / **handicraft** [ˋhændɪˌkræft] n. 手工藝品 / **foldable** [ˋfoldəbl̩] adj. 可摺疊的 / **touch** [tʌtʃ] n. 潤飾，潤色（在這裡指活動中額外增加的設施）/ **stall** [stɔl] n. 攤位 / **souvenir** [ˋsuvəˌnɪr] n. 紀念品

請用 1 分半的時間思考你對於以下問題的答案，然後用 1 分半的時間錄下你的回答。你可以用測驗卷做筆記並整理你的想法。

Have you tried watching movies via a streaming service? How is it different from going to a theater? Do you think movie theaters will still exist in the future? Please explain.

你嘗試過用串流服務看電影嗎？和去電影院有什麼不一樣？你認為電影院未來還會存在嗎？請說明。

**草稿擬定**

1. 說明使用串流服務（例如 Netflix）看電影的經驗和一些優點（或者缺點）。如果沒使用過，也可以說自己從別人口中得知的情況。
2. 說明在電影院看電影的優點（或者缺點），並且和串流服務做比較。
3. 針對串流服務是否將取代傳統電影院的問題，提出自己的看法以及理由。

**回答範例**

Yes, I watch movies on Netflix most of the time. On Netflix, I can watch movies in Full HD anytime I want. There are all kinds of movies there, such as horror, action, and romance, so I can always find something I'm interested in. There are so many movies to choose from, while movie theaters can only show a limited number of movies at one time. However, I do go to a theater sometimes, depending on the type of film. I think it's better to watch a horror movie or action movie in a theater, since there is equipment such as surround sound speakers and huge screens, which can make me feel immersed in a movie. Watching a movie on a TV screen just won't do the job. I also like to cry or scream with the audience. It's an incredible experience that so many people feel the same emotion together and at the same time. Therefore, even though many people now choose to watch movies at home, I think that movie theaters will still exist in the future. Watching movies isn't just about what we see on the screen. It's the feeling of being emotionally connected with others that makes the movie-going experience so special. By the way, many movie theaters in Taiwan have food courts, so after watching a movie with my friends, we can have a meal there and talk about the movie. I believe such a great place for social gathering will not disappear.

範例中譯

是的，我大多會在 Netflix 上看電影。在 Netflix 上，我可以隨時觀看超高畫質的電影。那裡有各種電影，例如驚悚、動作、浪漫愛情片，所以我總是能找到自己有興趣的東西。有很多電影可以選擇，而電影院只能同時放映數量有限的電影。不過，我有時候確實會去電影院，取決於電影的類型。我認為在電影院看驚悚片或動作片比較好，因為那裡有環繞音響和大型銀幕之類的設備，可以讓我感覺沉浸在電影中。在電視螢幕上看電影就是沒有這樣的效果。我也喜歡跟觀眾一起哭或尖叫。這麼多人同時一起感受到同樣的情緒，是非常棒的經驗。所以，儘管許多人現在選擇在家看電影，我認為電影院未來仍然會存在。看電影不止是關於我們在銀幕上看到的內容。是情緒上和其他人有所連結的感覺，才使得上電影院的經驗這麼特別。對了，台灣許多電影院有美食街，所以和我的朋友看了電影之後，我們可以在那邊用餐並且談論那部電影。我相信這麼好的社交聚會場所是不會消失的。

|單字片語| **Full HD (Full High Definition)** 超高畫質 / **surround sound speakers** 環繞音響 / **immerse** [ɪˋmɝs] v. 使沉浸 / **do the job** 起作用，有效 / **food court** （商場的）美食街

# 第四回　寫作能力測驗答題注意事項

1. 本測驗共有兩部分。第一部分為中譯英，第二部分為引導寫作。測驗時間為 **50 分鐘**。

2. 請利用試題紙空白處及背面擬稿，但正答務必書寫在「寫作能力測驗答案紙」上。在答案紙以外的地方作答，不予計分。

3. 第一部分中譯英請在答案紙第一頁開始作答，第二部分引導寫作請自答案紙第二頁起作答。

4. 作答時請勿隔行書寫，請注意字跡應清晰可讀，並請保持答案紙之清潔，以免影響評分。

5. 未獲監試人員指示前，請勿翻閱試卷。

6. 測驗時，不得在考試通知或其他物品上抄題，亦不得有傳遞、夾帶小抄、左顧右盼或交談等違規行為。

7. 意圖或已經將試卷攜出試場者，五年內不得報名參加本測驗。請人代考者，連同代考者，三年內不得報名參加本測驗。

8. 測驗結束時，須立即停止作答，在原位靜候監試人員收回全部試卷及答案紙，清點無誤後，宣佈結束始可離場。

9. 應試者入場、出場及測驗中如有違反上列規則或不服監試人員之指示者，監試人員得取消其應試資格並請其離場，且作答不予計分。

# 全民英語能力分級檢定測驗
## GENERAL ENGLISH PROFICIENCY TEST
## High-Intermediate Level Writing Test

**Part I: Chinese-English Translation (40%)**

Translate the following Chinese passage into an English passage, and write your answer on the Writing Test Answer Sheet.

足球是一種團隊運動。沒有一場比賽是單單由於個人的努力或天才而贏得的。所以，好的教練必須知道如何讓球員們團隊合作。每位球員都有特定的角色要扮演，而勝利的關鍵是合作。沒有團隊精神，即使是一隊有才華的明星球員，也有可能被相對沒沒無聞的隊伍打敗。

**Part II: Guided Writing (60%)**

Write an essay of **150~180 words** in an appropriate style on the following topic. Write your answer on the Writing Test Answer Sheet.

Both adults and teenagers can be addicted to smartphones. Many studies show that people spend a large portion of their time using smartphones for various reasons. In your essay, you should
(1) provide reasons why smartphones are highly addictive, and
(2) discuss the possible impact of spending too much time on smartphones.

# 全民英語能力檢定測驗

## 中高級寫作能力測驗答案紙

第一部分請由第 1 行開始作答，勿隔行書寫。第二部分請翻至第 2 頁作答。

1 _____

_____

_____

_____

5 _____

_____

_____

_____

_____

10 _____

_____

_____

_____

_____

15 _____

第二部分請翻至第 2 頁作答。

1 _____

_____

_____

_____

5 _____

_____

_____

_____

_____

10_____

_____

_____

_____

_____

15_____

_____

_____

_____

_____

20_____

45

50

55

60

# 第四回　口說能力測驗答題注意事項

1. 本測驗問題由耳機播放，回答則經麥克風錄下。分回答問題、看圖敘述與申述題三部份，時間共約 20 分鐘，連同口試說明時間共需約 50 分鐘。

2. 第一部份回答問題的題目只播出一次，聽完題目後請立即回答。第二部份看圖敘述有 30 秒的思考時間及 1 分 30 秒的答題時間；第三部份申述題分別有 1 分 30 秒的思考時間及答題時間。思考時，請不要發出聲音。等聽到指示開始回答時，請針對圖片或申述題的題目在作答時間內盡量的表達。

3. 錄音設備皆已事先完成設定，請勿觸動任何機件，以免影響錄音。測驗時請戴妥耳機，將麥克風調到嘴邊約三公分處，依指示以適中音量回答。

4. 測驗進行間，不可以在試題紙以外任何物品上書寫與測驗相關之任何文字、符號，亦不可有傳遞、夾帶小抄、左顧右盼或交談等違規行為，否則作答不予計分。

5. 意圖或已將試題紙或試題影音資料攜出或傳送出試場者，視同侵犯本中心著作財產權，限五年內不得報名參加「全民英檢」測驗。請人代考者，連同代考者，三年內不得報名參加本測驗。

6. 測驗結束時，須立即停止作答，在原位靜候監試人員收回全部試題紙並清點無誤，等候監試人員宣布結束後始可離場。

7. 入場、出場及測驗中如有違反上列規則或不服監試人員之指示者，監試人員將取消您的應試資格並請您離場，且測驗成績不予計分，亦不退費。

# 全民英語能力分級檢定測驗

GENERAL ENGLISH PROFICIENCY TEST

## High-Intermediate Level Speaking Test

**Please read the self-introduction sentence.**

My seat number is (座位號碼後 5 碼) , and my registration number is (考試號碼後 5 碼) .

### Part 1    Answering Questions

You will hear 8 questions. Each question will be spoken once. Please answer the question immediately after you hear it.

For questions 1 to 4, you will have 15 seconds to answer each question.

For questions 5 to 8, you will have 30 seconds to answer each question.

**Part II  Picture Description**

Look at the picture, think about the questions below for 30 seconds, and then record your answers for 1½ minutes.

1. Where was this picture probably taken? What makes you think so?
2. What do you think the people have been doing? Have you ever seen such kind of work in progress? Tell me about your experience.
3. What might have happened before these people arrived at the scene?
4. How would you feel if you saw such a scene in your neighborhood? Please explain.
5. If you still have time, please describe the picture in as much detail as you can.

## Part III    Discussion

Think about your answer(s) to the question(s) below for 1½ minutes, and then record your answer(s) for 1½ minutes. You may use your test paper to make notes and organize your ideas.

As the proportion of older people keeps increasing, what kinds of problems will our society and the elderly face? How can we prepare for our own life in old age? Please explain.

**Please read the self-introduction sentence again.**

My seat number is (座位號碼後 5 碼) , and my registration number is (考試號碼後 5 碼) .

# 複試 寫作測驗 解析

第 1 回
第 2 回
第 3 回
第 4 回
第 5 回
第 6 回

▶▶▶ 第一部分 **中譯英** (40%)

將以下這段中文翻譯成英文。

足球是一種團隊運動。沒有一場比賽是單單由於個人的努力或天才而贏得的。所以,好的教練必須知道如何讓球員們團隊合作。每位球員都有特定的角色要扮演,而勝利的關鍵是合作。沒有團隊精神,即使是一隊有才華的明星球員,也有可能被相對沒沒無聞的隊伍打敗。

**翻譯範例**

Soccer is a team sport. There is not a single match which is won solely due to an individual's effort or genius. Therefore, a good coach must know how to get the players to work as a team. Each player has a specific role to play, and the key to victory is cooperation. Without team spirit, even a team of talented star players can be defeated by a relatively obscure team.

**逐句說明**

## 1. 足球是一種團隊運動。

**Soccer is a team sport.**

• 這是很簡單的 be 動詞直述句,就連「團隊運動」也是逐字翻譯就好。有時候會出現 be 動詞的主詞和補語單複數不一致的情況,尤其是表示「複數主詞屬於某個種類」的句子,這時候 be 動詞的單複數和主詞一致,例如:「Bananas are a healthy food.(香蕉是一種健康的食物)」。

## 2. 沒有一場比賽是單單由於個人的努力或天才而贏得的。

**There is not a single match which is won solely due to**

an individual's effort or genius.

- 正式的書面語比較少使用口語式的略縮，所以這裡寫成 There is not 而不是 There's not / There isn't。
- 其實省略 single 這個字，意思也差不多，但用了 single 有特別強調「就連一個單獨的特例也沒有」的感覺。例如：「There isn't a single day that/when I don't think of you.（我沒有一天不想你）」。
- 足球的比賽可以翻譯成 match 或 game，match 這個字有「雙方競賽」的意涵。在英式英文中，通常會說足球比賽是 match 而不是 game。

## 3. 所以，好的教練必須知道如何讓球員們團隊合作。

Therefore, a good coach must know how to get the players to work as a team.

- 「所以」：Therefore。也可以用 Thus 或 Hence 來表達。
- get someone to do something 表示「促使某人做某事」，請注意後面用的是 to 不定詞。也可以簡單用 make 來翻譯：「... know how to make the players work as a team」，這時候就不會加 to。
- 「團隊合作」：work as a team。可能會有人想把這裡的「合作」翻成 cooperate，但其實 as a team（以團隊方式）就有「合作」的意思了，所以動詞可以簡單使用 work 就好。

## 4. 每位球員都有特定的角色要扮演，而勝利的關鍵是合作。

Each player has a specific role to play, and the key to victory is cooperation.

- 請記得 Each... 視為單數，動詞要使用單數形態，和 every...、everyone 是一樣的。
- 「扮演角色」：play a role。也可以說 perform a role 或 play a part。
- 「特定的」：specific。如果想不出這個字，也可以翻譯成 special（特別的），只是沒有那麼精準而已。
- 「…的關鍵」：key to...。請記得要使用介系詞 to。

5. 沒有團隊精神，即使是一隊有才華的明星球員，也有可能被相對沒沒無聞的隊伍打敗。

Without team spirit, even a team of talented star players can be defeated by a relatively obscure team.

- 「沒有…」：Without...。雖然也可以寫成 If there is no team spirit，但顯得不夠簡潔，也有過於口語之嫌。有一個比較適合書面語的說法是：「In the absence of...（在沒有…的情況下）」。

- 「團隊精神」：team spirit。因為這是一個固定的說法，所以只有靠著平時加強學習這類片語才能確實得分。如果真的不知道怎麼翻譯，也要想辦法變通，例如換成「the attitude of playing/working as a team」等意思差不多的說法。

- relatively 雖然是「相對地」的意思，但請小心後面的形容詞不使用比較級，而是用原級，例如 relatively easy、relatively cheap。這是因為 relatively 本身已經有「比較」的含意，再使用比較級的形容詞反而是多餘的。

- 「被…打敗」：be defeated by...。或者也可以說 be beat by...。

- 「沒沒無聞的」：obscure。不過，實際上可能不容易想到這個字，所以也可以翻譯成 little known 或 unknown。

▶▶▶  第二部分 引導寫作 (60%)

依照以下主題，以適當的文體寫一篇 150~180 字的短文。

Both adults and teenagers can be addicted to smartphones. Many studies show that people spend a large portion of their time using smartphones for various reasons. In your essay, you should
(1) provide reasons why smartphones are highly addictive, and
(2) discuss the possible impact of spending too much time on smartphones.

成人和青少年都有可能沉迷於智慧型手機。許多研究顯示，人們因為各種理由而花一大部分的時間使用智慧型手機。在你的短文中，你應該
(1) 提供智慧型手機之所以非常讓人上癮的理由，並且
(2) 討論花太多時間在智慧型手機上可能產生的影響。

## 草稿擬定

根據題目的提示，先設想大致上的文章結構，然後列舉自己想到的細節內容。這些內容可能沒辦法全部寫進文章，但可以作為寫作時的參考。

### 1. 智慧型手機之所以非常讓人上癮的理由

→ 多樣的手機遊戲：登入獎勵和特別活動
a wide variety of mobile games: login rewards and special events

→ 無窮的線上娛樂：電影、戲劇、動畫、小說、音樂…
endless entertainment online: movies, dramas, animations, novels, music...

→ 社群媒體：聊天、po 自拍照、更新動態、交友…
social media: chatting, posting selfies, updating status, making friends...

### 2. 花太多時間在智慧型手機上可能產生的影響

→ 浪費可以做更有意義的事情的時間
wasting time that can be used to do something more meaningful

→ 學生可能荒廢學業  students may neglect their studies

→ （工作）生產力與效率下降  a decrease in productivity and efficiency

→ 對家庭關係的負面影響  adverse effect on family relationship

→ 造成健康相關問題  lead to health-related problems

## 重點提示

• 有時候，即使想到了很多內容，還是很難想出文章開頭第一句話的切入方式。有一個方法是敘述大家共同的生活經驗，或者常見的社會現象，讓讀者能認同並產生共鳴，然後把話題推展到文章主要的內容。這裡的例文一開始先描述大家很熟悉的現象：隨處都可以看到每個人盯著手機螢幕，後面接著說明現代人有多麼依賴手機。

• 因為字數的關係，所以不打算太深入探討每個手機讓人上癮的理由，選擇「手機遊戲」和「社群媒體」這兩點，在第一段做簡要的描述。

第 1 回

第 2 回

第 3 回

第 4 回

第 5 回

第 6 回

- 同樣的，因為篇幅有限，所以第二段省略了「對家庭關係的負面影響」不談。

作文範例

①No matter where you are, whether in a restaurant or a train station, you will notice people who ②are glued to their smartphones. ③Apparently, ④smartphones have become indispensable for most of us, ⑤serving as a web browser, a schedule planner, a messaging device, etc. Meanwhile, "smartphone addiction" has become a problem for some. Every day they spend hours playing mobile games or checking social media. Mobile games are designed to ⑥keep their players occupied with ⑦a variety of login rewards and special events that take place at specific times of a day. Social apps, on the other hand, ⑧prompt their users to open them with all kinds of notifications.

Excessive use of smartphones means less time allocated for other tasks. ⑨There is no denying that smartphone usage has ⑩more or less taken up our time for more productive and constructive things. We can also see some students and working professionals' performance affected by smartphone addiction. ⑪ Moreover, overuse of smartphones also ⑫increases the risk of health-related problems such as nearsightedness and muscle pains. Therefore, we should just switch off our phones sometimes and get a life.

範例中譯

不管你在哪裡，是在餐廳或車站裡，你都會注意到眼睛盯著智慧型手機的人。顯然，智慧型手機對我們大部分的人來說已經不可或缺，它們可以是網路瀏覽器、行程計畫表、傳訊息的設備等等。同時，「智慧型手機成癮症」已經成為某些人的問題。他們每天花數小時玩手機遊戲或者查看社交媒體。手機遊戲被設計成用各種登入獎勵和每天特定時間的特別活動

讓玩家忙於進行遊戲。另一方面，社交 app 則是用各種通知提醒用戶打開程式。

　　過度使用智慧型手機意味著分配給其他工作的時間變少。不可否認，智慧型手機的使用或多或少佔據了我們做更有生產力、更有建設性的事情的時間。我們也可以看到一些學生和專業工作者的表現因為智慧型手機成癮症而受到影響。而且，過度使用智慧型手機也會增加近視、肌肉痠痛等健康相關問題的風險。所以，有時我們應該把手機關掉，做點有益的事。

## 文法分析與替換表達方式

① 如果只是要表達「不管你在哪裡」的話，其實只要寫成 No matter where you are, you will... 就好了。但是，如果像這裡一樣要追加舉例「不管是在 A 還是 B」的話，就會插入「whether... or...」。請注意前面使用了關係副詞 where，表示所在之處，所以 whether... or... 裡面是介系詞片語 in a restaurant、(in) a train station。如果前面是關係代名詞的話，whether... or... 裡面就會是名詞片語，例如：「No matter what you buy, whether a car or just a toy, you should compare prices.（不管你買什麼，是車子或只是玩具，你都應該比價）」。

② be glued to...（黏著…）。這裡是表示好像被黏在什麼上面，比喻「離不開」的意思。people who are glued to their smartphones 也可以說是 people who are absorbed in their smartphones（全神貫注於智慧型手機的人）或 people who keep looking at their smartphones。

③ Apparently 顯然 ≒ Obviously ≒ Evidently

④ smartphones have become indispensable 智慧型手機已經變得不可或缺

　　≒ smartphones have become something absolutely essential
　　智慧型手機已經成為絕對必要的東西

　　≒ smartphones have become something we can't live without
　　智慧型手機已經成為我們生活中不能沒有的東西

⑤ serving as... 的部分使用了分詞構句，這裡可以理解為 as they (smartphones) serve as... 的意思。或者也可以選擇在這個地方另起一句，用不同的句型表達智慧型手機的多功能，例如：Apart from the basic functions of a phone, a smartphone also serves as...（除了電話的基本功能以外，智慧型手機也能作為…）；Besides making and receiving calls, a smartphone can also be used as...（除了打電話、接電話以外，智慧型手機也能用為…）。

⑥ keep someone occupied（保持某人忙碌、做某事）。occupy 雖然是「佔據」的意思，但也可以引申為「佔用某個人的時間、精力」，通常會用被動態，例如 be occupied with something（忙於某事），或者用反身句型 occupy oneself with something（使自己忙於某事）。

⑦ a variety of...（各種各樣的…）≒ various types of ≒ all kinds of

⑧ prompt someone to do...（促使某人做…）。例如：「Advertisements are meant to prompt consumers to purchase more.（廣告的用意是促使消費者買得更多）」。

⑨ There is no denying that...（無可否認…）

　　≒ There is no doubt that...（無疑地…）

　　≒ Without (a) doubt, ...

⑩ more or less（或多或少）≒ to a certain extent（某個程度上）

⑪ Moreover（而且，此外）≒ Furthermore ≒ What's more ≒ In addition

⑫ increase the risk of health-related problems

　　增加健康相關問題的風險

　　≒ put your health at risk　危害你的健康

# 複試 口說測驗 解析

▶▶▶ 第一部分 回答問題

> 你會聽到 8 個問題。每個問題會唸一次。請在聽到題目後立刻回答。第 1 到第 4 題，每題有 15 秒可以回答。第 5 到第 8 題，每題有 30 秒可以回答。

## 1 Do you prefer to spend your weekends at home or outside? Please explain your choice.

你比較喜歡在家或者在外面度過週末？請說明你的選擇。

**答題策略**

1. 經過一週的工作之後，有些人認為應該在家好好休息，或者不想再出門奔波。但也有人認為，因為平日白天都待在職場，所以更要利用週末時間享受戶外的陽光。

2. 如果有多的時間，應該說明具體來說會做什麼事情，例如在家可以多睡一些（get extra sleep）、追劇（binge-watch series）、玩線上遊戲（play online games），在外面則可以上山健行（go hiking）、野餐（go on a picnic）、購物（go shopping）等等。

**回答範例 A**

I prefer to spend the weekend at home. I often work extra hours, and I don't sleep well, so I have to pay off my sleep debt on weekends. I usually sleep until noon and make myself a great brunch.

我偏好在家度過週末。我常常加班，而且我睡得不好，所以我週末必須還我的睡眠債。我通常會睡到中午，然後為我自己做一頓很棒的早午餐。

回答範例 B

I go outside whenever I can. After five days working in my office, the weekend is the only time I can enjoy the daylight outside, so I would go hiking to get in touch with nature.

只要可以的時候，我就會出門。在辦公室工作五天之後，週末是我唯一能在外面享受日光的時候，所以我會上山健行來接觸大自然。

## 2 Have you ever attended a baseball game? Tell me about your experience.

你曾經到場看過棒球比賽嗎？告訴我你的經驗。

### 答題策略

1. 如果有現場看棒球比賽的經驗，可以提到現場的氣氛（atmosphere/mood）、啦啦隊員（cheerleader）、食物和飲料（food and drink）、粉絲紀念品店（fan shop）等等。

2. 如果你不住在棒球場附近，或者根本不是棒球迷，很有可能從來沒去過球場。你可以轉述從朋友那邊聽來的經驗，或者談談自己在電視上看球賽轉播的印象。如果根本不看球賽，也可以說說自己沒興趣、不喜歡的原因。

回答範例 A

Yes, I've attended at least thirty games. I like watching games at a stadium, as I can see everything happening on the field, and I enjoy cheering together with fellow fans.

是的，我到場看過至少三十場比賽。我喜歡在球場看比賽，因為我可以看到場上發生的每件事，而且我喜歡和同隊球迷一起歡呼。

回答範例 B

No, but I've watched live games on TV. I'm not familiar with the rules, so it's informative to hear the commentator describe each play and event. I wouldn't know what's going on without the commentary.

沒有，但我看過電視上的現場轉播比賽。我不熟悉規則，所以聽到實況解說員描述（比賽中的）每個動作和發生的事情，能得到我所需要的資訊。沒有實況解說的話，我就不知道場上發生什麼事了。

|單字片語| **commentator** [ˋkɑmənˌtetɚ] **n.** 實況解說員 / **play** [ple] **n.** 比賽中的動作 / **commentary** [ˋkɑmənˌtɛrɪ] **n.** 實況解說

### 重點補充

露天並設有看台的運動場地，例如棒球場、田徑場、足球場等等，通常稱為 stadium。而建築結構比較完整，觀眾席在四周圍繞中間場地的體育館，通常稱為 arena（例如台北小巨蛋），可以用來舉辦籃球、排球賽或演唱會等等。至於運動員比賽時的活動範圍，棒球、足球稱為 field，籃球、排球、網球、羽毛球稱為 court。

## 3 Your friend Alice works as a receptionist at a financial firm. Ask her some questions about her job.

你朋友 Alice 在金融機構當接待員。問一些關於她工作的問題。

### 答題策略

1. 關鍵字為 receptionist（接待員或電話總機人員）和 financial firm（金融機構）。除了問一些常見的問題，也必須提到關於金融或投資理財的細節，讓考官知道你完全理解題目，並且能做出適當的回應。

2. 你也可以半開玩笑地問對方，是否聽說過什麼投資建議（Have you heard of any investment recommendation?），或者有沒有在股市中大撈一筆（Have you made a killing in the stock market?）。

**回答範例** A

Isn't it boring to answer the phone all day? What else do you have to do? Do you get tips on what stocks to buy? If you don't mind, could you tell me your monthly salary and year-end bonus?

一整天接電話不是很無聊嗎？你還有什麼必須做的？你會得到關於要買什麼股票的內部消息嗎？如果你不介意的話，可以告訴我你的月薪和年終獎金（多少）嗎？

**回答範例** B

Are there more men than women in your firm? Is it true that stockbrokers make a lot of money? What kind of calls do you usually get? What do you do if there are no incoming calls?

你的機構裡男人比女人多嗎？證券經紀人賺很多錢是真的嗎？你通常接到什麼樣的電話？沒有電話的時候你做什麼？

|單字片語| **receptionist** [rɪ`sɛpʃənɪst] n. 接待員 / **financial firm** 金融機構 / **tip** [tɪp] n. 指點，提示；（投資、賭博等的）內部消息，祕密消息 / **year-end bonus** 年終獎金 / **stockbroker** [`stɑk͵brokɚ] n. 證券經紀人 / **incoming call** 打來的電話（ ⟷ **outgoing call** 打出去的電話）

4 **Your mother asks you to help with spring cleaning before Chinese New Year. Tell her how you plan to clean the house.**

**你媽媽要你幫忙進行春節前的大掃除。告訴她你打算怎麼清掃房子。**

**答題策略**

1. 大掃除的計畫，主要是關於誰做什麼，還有什麼是優先的事情（priorities）。為了不讓媽媽過於勞累，你也可以提出雇用別人（hire someone）幫忙的建議。

2. 除了一般的打掃之外，也可以提出一些美化房子的建議，例如粉刷牆壁（paint the walls）之類的。

回答範例 A

Mom, I have to work overtime the week before Chinese New Year because that is the busiest time in the shop. Why don't we pay someone to do the spring cleaning for us?

媽，我過年前一週要加班，因為那是店裡最忙的時候。我們何不花錢請人幫忙大掃除呢？

回答範例 B

All right, Mom. I'll start with my room. I'll make sure it's clean and tidy. Then I'll help you wipe the windows and mop the floor. You might have to decide what to discard because we're running out of space.

好，媽。我會從我房間開始。我一定會讓房間乾淨又整齊。然後我會幫你擦窗戶、拖地板。你可能必須決定要丟掉什麼，因為我們的空間快不夠了。

|單字片語| **spring cleaning** 春季大掃除 / **work overtime** 加班工作 / **make sure** 確保… / **discard** [dɪsˋkɑrd] v. 拋棄，丟棄

---

**5** **Why do you think some parents prefer not to let their children use smartphones?**

**你覺得為什麼有些父母比較希望不讓小孩用智慧型手機？**

答題策略

有了智慧型手機，很多學生會沉迷於手機（be addicted to their smartphones）而花掉很多寶貴的時間。父母擔心這樣會影響孩子的學習。健康是父母擔憂的另一個因素，他們可能擔心孩子會近視（will become nearsighted）或近視加深（nearsightedness will get worse）。

回答範例 A

I will not let my kids use a smartphone until they finish senior high school. Many parents finally realize how addictive and destructive smartphones can be. If children spend too much time using smartphones, they won't have enough time for their schoolwork. As a result, their grades will be badly affected.

我不會讓我的小孩在高中畢業之前用智慧型手機。許多家長最後了解到智慧型手機會有多麼令人上癮而且有害。如果小孩花太多時間用智慧型手機，他們不會有足夠的時間做學校的功課。結果，他們的成績會嚴重受到影響。

回答範例 B

For children who lack self-control and discipline, smartphones can cause a lot of harm. For one, it may create health problems such as nearsightedness. For another, students may lose interest in their schoolwork. Last but not least, spending too much time using smartphones is harmful to family relationships.

對於缺乏自制與紀律的兒童而言，智慧型手機可能造成許多傷害。首先，它可能造成近視之類的健康問題。再者，學生可能對功課失去興趣。最後同樣重要的是，花太多時間使用智慧型手機對家人的關係有害。

|單字片語| **addictive** [ə`dɪktɪv] adj. 令人上癮的 / **destructive** [dɪ`strʌktɪv] adj. 破壞的，毀滅性的 / **schoolwork** [`skul͵wɝk] n. 學業；功課 / **self-control** [͵sɛlfkən`trol] n. 自制 / **nearsightedness** [`nɪr`saɪtɪdnɪs] n. 近視

**If you were going to make a donation, what factors would you consider important when choosing a charity to support?**

如果你要捐款的話，在選擇要支持的慈善機構時，你認為什麼因素是重要的？

**答題策略**

選擇慈善團體，最重要的是民眾的捐款是否花在刀口上（whether the donation is spent on what's important），是否讓需要的人受惠（whether the donation benefits those in need）。因此，這些團體的名譽（reputation）很重要。你可以說你認識某個志工（volunteer），從他的口中得知某個機構真的有在做事，所以你會考慮捐款。再者是機構幫助的對象，可以提出你個人比較喜歡幫助的弱勢，例如老人、小孩或病人。除了人，你也可以幫助流浪動物（stray animals）。

回答範例 A

The most important thing is honesty. The charity has to be transparent in the way funds are spent. I don't want to see the money I donate being used on something unrelated to charity. Another factor is the people the organization is helping. I'm more sympathetic to people with a terminal illness. Once I donated some money to help children with bone cancer.

最重要的是誠實。這家慈善機構使用資金時必須透明。我不想看到自己捐的錢被用在與慈善無關的事物。另一個因素是這個組織幫助的人。我比較同情末期病人。我有一次捐錢幫助有骨癌的兒童。

回答範例 B

I helped to raise funds for an orphanage as part of my volunteer work in junior high school. The money we collected was used to purchase food and basic necessities for the children. I will support charities that do something meaningful to help the needy. One more thing, I will not donate money to organizations that have a bad reputation.

我在國中做志工服務時曾經幫孤兒院募款。我們募集的錢是用來為那些小孩購買食物和基本必需品。我會支持做有意義的事情幫助窮困者的慈善機構。還有，我不會捐錢給名聲不好的機構。

|單字片語| **make a donation** 捐款，捐贈 / **charity** [ˋtʃærətɪ] n. （不可數）慈善；（可數）慈善機構 / **honesty** [ˋɑnɪstɪ] n. 誠實 / **transparent** [trænsˋpɛrənt] adj. 透明的；坦白的 / **sympathetic** [ˌsɪmpəˋθɛtɪk] adj. 同情的 / **terminal** [ˋtɝmən!] adj. 終點的；末期的 / **raise funds for** 為…募集資金 / **orphanage** [ˋɔrfənɪdʒ] n. 孤兒院 / **necessity** [nəˋsɛsətɪ] n. 必需品 / **needy** [ˋnidɪ] adj. 窮困的 / **reputation** [ˌrɛpjəˋteʃən] n. 名聲

7 **What are the benefits or drawbacks of taking public transportation, compared with driving a car?**

和開車比起來，搭乘大眾運輸工具有什麼優點或缺點？

**答題策略**

主要說明交通工具的利與弊。例如捷運系統方便、可靠、沒有塞車問題、便宜而快速，缺點是尖峰時間（rush hours）會很擁擠、不舒服。相對之下，開車比較自由，也可以去一些捷運到不了的地方。而且，除了大台北地區以外，其他地區的大眾運輸還不夠全面（extensive），因此很多人還是用汽車或機車代步。

回答範例 A

My workplace is accessible by MRT, so I take public transportation to work. One of the benefits is that I don't have to worry about getting caught in traffic jams. Driving can be frustrating in a crowded city like Taipei. Parking is also a big problem. And let us not forget that taking the MRT helps to reduce air pollution.

我工作的地方搭捷運可以到，所以我搭大眾運輸工具上班。優點之一是我不必擔心遇到塞車。在像台北這樣擁擠的城市，開車可能會讓人很洩氣。停車也是個大問題。還有我們別忘了搭捷運有助於減少空氣污染。

There is only one direct bus route to my school. If I miss a bus, I have to wait for twenty to thirty minutes. My dad drives me to school because it is much more convenient, especially on rainy days. I understand that taking public transportation is good for the environment. However, it is not a viable option in my case.

只有一條公車路線可以直接到我的學校。如果我錯過一台公車，我就要等二、三十分鐘。我爸開車載我上學，因為這樣方便多了，尤其在下雨天。我明白搭乘大眾運輸工具對環境有益。不過，以我的情況來說不是可行的選項。

|單字片語| **public transportation** 大眾運輸（工具） / **workplace** [`wɝk͵ples] n. 工作場所 / **frustrating** [`frʌstretɪŋ] adj. 令人洩氣的，令人心煩的 / **viable** [`vaɪəbl] adj. 可行的

8 **Do you think being a woman is a disadvantage in the business world today? Please explain.**
在今日的商業界，你認為身為女性是不利的條件嗎？請說明。

答題策略

無可否認，商場上男性居多。然而，這對女性來說反而是一種優勢（advantage）。在這個講究性別平等（gender equality）的時代，職業婦女（career women）的能力是受到肯定的。當然，有些人還是對女性有偏見（have a bias against women）。你也可以用自己身邊一些成功女性的例子來支持你的論點。

The answer is definitely "no". Nowadays, career women are highly respected in the business world. Many CEOs are women with outstanding leadership skills. In fact, women have some advantages over men because they are generally more observant and tolerant, and they have a higher emotional intelligence. There are many women who are successful today.

答案當然是「不」。現在職業婦女在商業界非常受到尊重。有許多執行長是具有傑出領導技巧的女性。事實上，女性有一些勝過男性的優勢，因為她們通常比較善於觀察、寬容，而且她們的情緒智商比較高。今日有許多很成功的女性。

### 回答範例 B

Despite talks about gender equality, I believe men and women can never be equal. In particular, the business world is biased against women. With the same qualifications and experience, men tend to receive a higher pay than women. Some employers are worried that women may get pregnant and go on leave. Some bosses are even of the opinion that women are inferior.

撇開關於性別平等的談論，我相信男女永遠不會是對等的。尤其商業界對女性有偏見。當資格和經驗相同時，男性得到的薪資通常比女性高。有些雇主擔心女人可能懷孕並且休假。甚至有些老闆認為女性比較低下。

|單字片語| **disadvantage** [ˌdɪsədˋvæntɪdʒ] n. 不利條件，不利情況 / **career woman** 職業婦女 / **leadership** [ˋlidɚˌʃɪp] n. 領導，領導力 / **observant** [əbˋzɝvənt] adj. 善於觀察的 / **tolerant** [ˋtɑlərənt] adj. 寬容的 / **emotional intelligence** 情緒智商 / **gender equality** 性別平等 / **be biased against** 對…有偏見 / **qualification** [ˌkwɑləfəˋkeʃən] n. 資格，資格證明 / **pregnant** [ˋprɛgnənt] adj. 懷孕的 / **go on leave** 休假 / **be of the opinion that** 認為… / **inferior** [ɪnˋfɪrɪɚ] adj. 比較低下的

請看照片，用 30 秒的時間思考以下問題，然後用 1 分半的時間錄下你的回答。

1. Where was this picture probably taken? What makes you think so?
2. What do you think the people have been doing? Have you ever seen such kind of work in progress? Tell me about your experience.
3. What might have happened before these people arrived at the scene?
4. How would you feel if you saw such a scene in your neighborhood? Please explain.
5. If you still have time, please describe the picture in as much detail as you can.

1. 這張照片可能是在哪裡拍的？為什麼你這麼認為？
2. 你認為這些人之前在做什麼？你看過這種工作進行中的情況嗎？告訴我你的經驗。
3. 這些人到現場之前可能發生了什麼事？
4. 你在自己家附近看到這種情景會有什麼感覺？請說明。
5. 如果你還有時間，請盡量詳細描述這張照片。

**草稿擬定**

1. 解釋圖中最醒目的重型機具（不必思考最精確的單字是什麼，因為考官並不期望你會知道非常專門的用語，你可以說這是一台 construction vehicle〔建設工程車輛〕就好，如果有餘力再描述它的細節）
2. 描述圖中的景象
3. 猜測之前可能發生的事情
4. 說明左上角三名男子的身分
5. 針對天災或拆除舊建築提出感想

**加分延伸**

關於拆除場景的想法，除了噪音以外，也可以說很多房子是自己從小看到大的，所以每次拆除就好像失去了一個記憶中的場景，感覺很可惜等等。

**回答範例**

In the middle of the picture, I see an excavator. I beg your pardon. It's not an excavator, but some kind of heavy-duty vehicle with a specially-designed arm to cut metal or carry objects. I also notice large pieces of broken concrete lying around. There are also thick steel bars on the left side of the picture. I'm not sure what happened. One possibility is that an earthquake caused a building to collapse. Another possibility is that the owner of the house decided to tear it down and build a new one on the site. I have a feeling that this is a construction site and not a disaster scene. I don't see any casualties, and there are no rescue dogs or ambulances in the background. The operator of the vehicle is trying to move some of the steel bars. I think it takes a lot of training to operate such a machine. There are three men on the top left corner of the picture. They're all wearing safety helmets and vests. They seem to be engaged in an important discussion. I used to hate the noise created when machines were used to demolish buildings. My uncle told me to put myself in the shoes of people working on site. If I could't stand the jarring noise from a few blocks away, what about those workers? What he said changed my perspective. Instead of complaining about the noise, I learned to respect people who have to endure the stress of working in such an environment.

範例中譯

在照片中間，我看到一台挖土機。抱歉。不是挖土機，是某種重型車輛，有特別設計的手臂可以切斷金屬或搬動物體。我也注意到四處散落的大型水泥碎塊。照片左邊還有粗的鋼筋。我不確定發生了什麼。一個可能是地震造成建築物倒塌。另一個可能是屋主決定拆房子，並且在原地重新蓋房子。我感覺這是工地而不是災難現場。我沒看到傷亡者，背景也沒有救難犬或救護車。操作這台車輛的人正試圖移動一些鋼筋。我想需要許多訓練才能操作這種機械。照片左上角有三個男人。他們都戴安全帽、穿著背心。他們看起來正在進行重要的討論。我以前很討厭用機械拆除建築物發出的噪音。我叔叔告訴我要從工地工人的立場著想。如果我受不了幾個街區外的刺耳噪音，那工人們呢？他說的話改變了我的觀點。我學到不要抱怨噪音，而要尊敬必須忍受這種環境裡的工作壓力的人。

|單字片語| **in progress** 進行中 / **excavator** [ˋɛkskəˌvetɚ] n. 挖掘機，挖土機 / **heavy-duty** [ˋhɛvɪˋdjutɪ] adj. 重型的 / **concrete** [ˋkɑnkrit] n. 混凝土，水泥 / **steel bar** 鋼條，鋼筋 / **tear down** 拆除… / **construction site** 工地 / **casualty** [ˋkæʒjʊəltɪ] n. 死者或傷者 / **rescue dog** 救難犬 / **safety helmet** 安全帽 / **be engaged in** 忙於…，從事… / **demolish** [dɪˋmɑlɪʃ] v. 拆除 / **put oneself in someone's shoes** 設身處地，從某人的角度著想 / **jarring** [ˋdʒɑrɪŋ] adj. 刺耳的 / **perspective** [pɚˋspɛktɪv] n. 觀點

### 第三部分 申述

請用 1 分半的時間思考你對於以下問題的答案，然後用 1 分半的時間錄下你的回答。你可以用測驗卷做筆記並整理你的想法。

As the proportion of older people keeps increasing, what kinds of problems will our society and the elderly face? How can we prepare for our own life in old age? Please explain.

隨著老年人比例持續增長，我們的社會和老年人會面臨什麼樣的問題？我們可以為自己的老年生活做什麼準備？請說明。

**草稿擬定**

1. 人口老化的問題主要是醫療照顧（medical care）的部分
2. 必須提供對年長者友善的公共設施（public facilities）
3. 我們不能期待政府和兒女的幫助，必須自己想辦法

**回答範例**

A rapidly aging population poses several problems for society. Among the problems, health care for the elderly is probably the greatest challenge. The government will have to reallocate resources so that the elderly can obtain the best medical care. A shortage of nurses is another concern. Old folks who are bedridden or confined to wheelchairs will need someone to take care of them. From what I know, many families have no choice but to turn to foreign workers because there are not enough qualified Taiwanese nurses. There is also a need to build more homes for the elderly. In Japan, many elderly-friendly policies were introduced to deal with the aging population. For example, public restrooms should be equipped with special handles and emergency buttons. Some supermarkets provide carts with attached magnifying glasses so the elderly can read labels clearly. When it comes to preparing for old age, the most important thing will be staying healthy. As long as our bodies remain strong and our minds sharp, we can still make a contribution to society as we grow old. Doing volunteer work after retirement is not only a good way to make new friends, but it also gives us a sense of purpose and satisfaction. It might be a good idea to develop new interests, such as learning a foreign language or playing a musical instrument.

### 範例中譯

快速老化的人口，對於社會有幾個問題。在這些問題中，老年人的醫療保健可能是最大的挑戰。政府將必須重新分配資源，讓老年人可以獲得最好的醫療。護士不足是另一個擔憂。臥病在床或受限於輪椅的老人會需要有人照顧他們。就我所知，許多家庭別無選擇，只能求助於外籍工作者，因為合格的台灣護士不夠。也有需要為老年人建設更多房屋。日本採用了許多對老年人友善的政策來應對人口老化。舉例來說，公廁應配備特別的把手和緊急按鈕。有些超市提供附放大鏡的推車，讓老年人可以把標籤看清楚。至於為老年做準備，最重要的是保持健康。只要身體維持強健、頭腦保持清楚，那麼我們變老的時候還是可以貢獻社會。退休後擔任志工不但是交新朋友的好方法，也能帶給我們目的感（有目標的感覺）和滿足感。發展新的興趣可能是個好主意，例如學外語或演奏樂器。

|單字片語| age [edʒ] v. 變老，老化 / population [ˌpɑpjəˋleʃən] n. 人口 / pose a problem 造成問題 / health care 醫療保健 / reallocate [riˋæləˌket] v. 重新分配 / medical care 醫療 / folks [foks] n. （口語）人們 / bedridden [ˋbɛdrɪdn̩] 臥病在床的 / have no choice but to do 除了做⋯別無選擇 / qualified [ˋkwɑləˌfaɪd] adj. 有資格的，合格的 / public restroom 公廁（美式說法，英國通常稱為 public toilet） / magnifying glass 放大鏡

# 第五回　寫作能力測驗答題注意事項

1. 本測驗共有兩部分。第一部分為中譯英，第二部分為引導寫作。測驗時間為 **50 分鐘**。

2. 請利用試題紙空白處及背面擬稿，但正答務必書寫在「寫作能力測驗答案紙」上。在答案紙以外的地方作答，不予計分。

3. 第一部分中譯英請在答案紙第一頁開始作答，第二部分引導寫作請自答案紙第二頁起作答。

4. 作答時請勿隔行書寫，請注意字跡應清晰可讀，並請保持答案紙之清潔，以免影響評分。

5. 未獲監試人員指示前，請勿翻閱試卷。

6. 測驗時，不得在考試通知或其他物品上抄題，亦不得有傳遞、夾帶小抄、左顧右盼或交談等違規行為。

7. 意圖或已經將試卷攜出試場者，五年內不得報名參加本測驗。請人代考者，連同代考者，三年內不得報名參加本測驗。

8. 測驗結束時，須立即停止作答，在原位靜候監試人員收回全部試卷及答案紙，清點無誤後，宣佈結束始可離場。

9. 應試者入場、出場及測驗中如有違反上列規則或不服監試人員之指示者，監試人員得取消其應試資格並請其離場，且作答不予計分。

# 全民英語能力分級檢定測驗
## GENERAL ENGLISH PROFICIENCY TEST

## High-Intermediate Level Writing Test

### Part I: Chinese-English Translation (40%)

Translate the following Chinese passage into an English passage, and write your answer on the Writing Test Answer Sheet.

　　有時候，觀看新聞可能對你的心理健康不好。由於媒體傾向於聚焦在災難和悲劇，新聞可能讓你覺得世界失去控制。一項研究發現，觀看了一些負面新聞的人會有比較高的壓力水平以及焦慮的症狀。所以，為了減少與新聞有關的壓力，你可以設法限制你所觀看的新聞的量。儘管知道當前的事件很重要，但這並不意味著你應該讓它們控制你的心情。

### Part II: Guided Writing (60%)

Write an essay of **150~180 words** in an appropriate style on the following topic. Write your answer on the Writing Test Answer Sheet.

A recent survey shows that 70% of its interviewees think that they are under a great deal of stress. Since it is virtually impossible to eliminate stress in our life, coping with stress is essential to both health and success. In your essay, you should
(1) identify the main sources or causes of stress, and
(2) provide suggestion(s) on how to reduce and relieve stress.

第一部分請由第 1 行開始作答，勿隔行書寫。第二部分請翻至第 2 頁作答。

1 _____

_____

_____

_____

5 _____

_____

_____

_____

_____

10 _____

_____

_____

_____

_____

15 _____

第二部分請翻至第 2 頁作答。

1 ＿＿＿＿＿＿＿＿＿＿＿＿＿＿＿＿＿＿＿＿＿＿＿＿＿＿＿＿＿＿＿＿

＿＿＿＿＿＿＿＿＿＿＿＿＿＿＿＿＿＿＿＿＿＿＿＿＿＿＿＿＿＿＿＿＿

＿＿＿＿＿＿＿＿＿＿＿＿＿＿＿＿＿＿＿＿＿＿＿＿＿＿＿＿＿＿＿＿＿

＿＿＿＿＿＿＿＿＿＿＿＿＿＿＿＿＿＿＿＿＿＿＿＿＿＿＿＿＿＿＿＿＿

5 ＿＿＿＿＿＿＿＿＿＿＿＿＿＿＿＿＿＿＿＿＿＿＿＿＿＿＿＿＿＿＿＿

＿＿＿＿＿＿＿＿＿＿＿＿＿＿＿＿＿＿＿＿＿＿＿＿＿＿＿＿＿＿＿＿＿

＿＿＿＿＿＿＿＿＿＿＿＿＿＿＿＿＿＿＿＿＿＿＿＿＿＿＿＿＿＿＿＿＿

＿＿＿＿＿＿＿＿＿＿＿＿＿＿＿＿＿＿＿＿＿＿＿＿＿＿＿＿＿＿＿＿＿

＿＿＿＿＿＿＿＿＿＿＿＿＿＿＿＿＿＿＿＿＿＿＿＿＿＿＿＿＿＿＿＿＿

10＿＿＿＿＿＿＿＿＿＿＿＿＿＿＿＿＿＿＿＿＿＿＿＿＿＿＿＿＿＿＿＿

＿＿＿＿＿＿＿＿＿＿＿＿＿＿＿＿＿＿＿＿＿＿＿＿＿＿＿＿＿＿＿＿＿

＿＿＿＿＿＿＿＿＿＿＿＿＿＿＿＿＿＿＿＿＿＿＿＿＿＿＿＿＿＿＿＿＿

＿＿＿＿＿＿＿＿＿＿＿＿＿＿＿＿＿＿＿＿＿＿＿＿＿＿＿＿＿＿＿＿＿

＿＿＿＿＿＿＿＿＿＿＿＿＿＿＿＿＿＿＿＿＿＿＿＿＿＿＿＿＿＿＿＿＿

15＿＿＿＿＿＿＿＿＿＿＿＿＿＿＿＿＿＿＿＿＿＿＿＿＿＿＿＿＿＿＿＿

＿＿＿＿＿＿＿＿＿＿＿＿＿＿＿＿＿＿＿＿＿＿＿＿＿＿＿＿＿＿＿＿＿

＿＿＿＿＿＿＿＿＿＿＿＿＿＿＿＿＿＿＿＿＿＿＿＿＿＿＿＿＿＿＿＿＿

＿＿＿＿＿＿＿＿＿＿＿＿＿＿＿＿＿＿＿＿＿＿＿＿＿＿＿＿＿＿＿＿＿

＿＿＿＿＿＿＿＿＿＿＿＿＿＿＿＿＿＿＿＿＿＿＿＿＿＿＿＿＿＿＿＿＿

20＿＿＿＿＿＿＿＿＿＿＿＿＿＿＿＿＿＿＿＿＿＿＿＿＿＿＿＿＿＿＿＿

25

30

35

40

45

50

55

60

# 第五回　口說能力測驗答題注意事項

1. 本測驗問題由耳機播放，回答則經麥克風錄下。分回答問題、看圖敘述與申述題三部份，時間共約 20 分鐘，連同口試說明時間共需約 50 分鐘。

2. 第一部份回答問題的題目只播出一次，聽完題目後請立即回答。第二部份看圖敘述有 30 秒的思考時間及 1 分 30 秒的答題時間；第三部份申述題分別有 1 分 30 秒的思考時間及答題時間。思考時，請不要發出聲音。等聽到指示開始回答時，請針對圖片或申述題的題目在作答時間內盡量的表達。

3. 錄音設備皆已事先完成設定，請勿觸動任何機件，以免影響錄音。測驗時請戴妥耳機，將麥克風調到嘴邊約三公分處，依指示以適中音量回答。

4. 測驗進行間，不可以在試題紙以外任何物品上書寫與測驗相關之任何文字、符號，亦不可有傳遞、夾帶小抄、左顧右盼或交談等違規行為，否則作答不予計分。

5. 意圖或已將試題紙或試題影音資料攜出或傳送出試場者，視同侵犯本中心著作財產權，限五年內不得報名參加「全民英檢」測驗。請人代考者，連同代考者，三年內不得報名參加本測驗。

6. 測驗結束時，須立即停止作答，在原位靜候監試人員收回全部試題紙並清點無誤，等候監試人員宣布結束後始可離場。

7. 入場、出場及測驗中如有違反上列規則或不服監試人員之指示者，監試人員將取消您的應試資格並請您離場，且測驗成績不予計分，亦不退費。

# 全民英語能力分級檢定測驗
## GENERAL ENGLISH PROFICIENCY TEST
## High-Intermediate Level Speaking Test

**Please read the self-introduction sentence.**

My seat number is (座位號碼後 5 碼) , and my registration number is (考試號碼後 5 碼) .

### Part 1　Answering Questions

You will hear 8 questions. Each question will be spoken once. Please answer the question immediately after you hear it.

For questions 1 to 4, you will have 15 seconds to answer each question.

For questions 5 to 8, you will have 30 seconds to answer each question.

## Part II  Picture Description

Look at the picture, think about the questions below for 30 seconds, and then record your answers for 1½ minutes.

1. Where was this picture probably taken? What makes you think so?
2. What are the people doing? Have you ever been in a similar situation? Tell me about your experience.
3. What may be the reason that the vehicle on the left side of the road is adopted in this place?
4. Do you think this kind of vehicle is ideal for your hometown? Please explain.
5. If you still have time, please describe the picture in as much detail as you can.

## Part III Discussion

Think about your answer(s) to the question(s) below for 1½ minutes, and then record your answer(s) for 1½ minutes. You may use your test paper to make notes and organize your ideas.

Electric cars are getting more and more popular these years. What are some benefits of electric cars, and what should be improved to make them more appealing to people? Please explain.

**Please read the self-introduction sentence again.**

My seat number is (座位號碼後 5 碼) , and my registration number is (考試號碼後 5 碼) .

# 複試 寫作測驗 解析

▶▶▶ 第一部分 中譯英 (40%)

將以下這段中文翻譯成英文。

有時候,觀看新聞可能對你的心理健康不好。由於媒體傾向於聚焦在災難和悲劇,新聞可能讓你覺得世界失去控制。一項研究發現,觀看了一些負面新聞的人會有比較高的壓力水平以及焦慮的症狀。所以,為了減少與新聞有關的壓力,你可以設法限制你所觀看的新聞的量。儘管知道當前的事件很重要,但這並不意味著你應該讓它們控制你的心情。

**翻譯範例**

Sometimes, watching the news can be bad for your mental health. Since the media tends to focus on disasters and tragedies, the news can make you feel that the world is out of control. A study found that those who have watched some negative news will have higher stress levels and symptoms of anxiety. Therefore, [in order] to reduce news-related stress, you can try to limit the amount of news you watch. Even though it is important to know current events, it does not mean you should let them control your mood.

**逐句說明**

### 1. 有時候,觀看新聞可能對你的心理健康不好。

Sometimes, watching the news can be bad for your mental health.

- 中文「觀看」提示要用 watch 這個動詞,表示看電視或者影片形式的新聞。

- watch the news 加冠詞 the 的情況遠比不加冠詞普遍,或許是因為 news

被視為各種新聞管道的總稱，而且是每個人日常生活中已經熟知的一部分。

- 這一句和下一句的「可能」翻譯成 can 或 may 都可以。
- 雖然「心理健康」翻譯成 psychological health 也不算錯，但絕大多數的情況會用 mental health 來表達。mental 的意思是「精神上的」。

## 2. 由於媒體傾向於聚焦在災難和悲劇，新聞可能讓你覺得世界失去控制。

Since the media tends to focus on disasters and tragedies, the news can make you feel that the world is out of control.

- 傳統上，media 被視為 medium 的複數形，所以動詞應該用複數形 tend，但在現代英語中，media 經常當成單數名詞使用，所以動詞用單數形 tends 也是正確的。
- 請記得「傾向於…」的英語說法是 tend to do。
- 因為是泛指各種災難和悲劇，所以 disaster 和 tragedy 都要加 -s。
- 「失控」用 be out of control（在控制之外）來表達。有些人可能會翻譯成 the world has lost control，但這樣表達其實有點不自然，因為 lose control 的主詞通常是有自由意志的人或動物，而 the world 通常被看成各種事件發生的地方，而不是有意識地做出行動的主體。

## 3. 一項研究發現，觀看了一些負面新聞的人會有比較高的壓力水平以及焦慮的症狀。

A study found that those who have watched some negative news will have higher stress levels and symptoms of anxiety.

- 「…的人」用 those who... 來表達，表示符合某種條件的不特定複數對象。如果忘了這個表達方式，換成 people who... 也可以。
- 因為這裡表達的是「因為現在已經有觀看負面新聞的經驗，而產生壓力和焦慮」，所以用現在完成式 have watched 會比簡單過去式來得恰當。
- 因為主詞 those 是複數，而每個人的壓力水平多少有些不同，所以 stress levels 使用複數形。

4. 所以，為了減少與新聞有關的壓力，你可以設法限制你所觀看的新聞的量。

Therefore, [in order] to reduce news-related stress, you can try to limit the amount of news you watch.

- 「與新聞有關的壓力」雖然也可以說是 stress related to news，但比較常見的表達方式是使用複合形容詞 news-related，讓文字顯得比較簡潔。類似的說法還有 computer-related jobs（和電腦相關的工作）等等。
- 「設法」只要用最簡單的 try to do 就能表達。另外，請注意 try doing 是「試試看」的意思，而不是像 try to do 一樣表示積極做到某件事。

5. 儘管知道當前的事件很重要，但這並不意味著你應該讓它們控制你的心情。

Even though it is important to know current events, it does not mean you should let them control your mood.

- 「當前的事件」是 current events，current 表示「現在發生中」的意思。請注意副詞 now 不能用來修飾名詞 events。
- 中文的「但」不能直接翻譯出來，因為 though 不能和 but 連用。
- 「它們」已經提示要用 them 來表達，而 them 指的是前面的 events。
- mood 雖然是很簡單的字，但看著中文不見得能想到。如果想不起來的話，也可以改用 feelings 來表達。

▶▶▶ 第二部分 引導寫作 (60%)

依照以下主題，以適當的文體寫一篇 150~180 字的短文。

A recent survey shows that 70% of its interviewees think that they are under a great deal of stress. Since it is virtually impossible to eliminate stress in our life, coping with stress is essential to both health and success. In your essay, you should
(1) identify the main sources or causes of stress, and
(2) provide suggestion(s) on how to reduce and relieve stress.

最近一項調查顯示，有 70% 的受訪者認為自己壓力很大。因為幾乎不可能去除我們生活中的壓力，所以處理壓力對於健康和成功都是必要的。在你的短文中，你應該

(1) 找出壓力的主要來源或成因，並且

(2) 提供減少及緩和壓力的建議。

**草稿擬定**

根據題目的提示，先設想大致上的文章結構，然後列舉自己想到的細節內容。這些內容可能沒辦法全部寫進文章，但可以作為寫作時的參考。

## 1. 壓力的來源和原因

→ 很難實現（別人的）期望 hard to live up to expectations

→ 過重的工作量 heavy workload

→ 緊繃的（工作等）日程安排 tight schedule

→ 總是趕著在期限之前完成工作
always rushing to complete work before deadlines

→ 與同儕、同事或主管間的人際關係問題
relationship problems with peers, colleagues, or supervisors

→ 夢想與現實的差距 the gap between dreams and reality

## 2. 減少及緩和壓力的建議

→ 採取正面積極的心態 adopt a positive mindset

→ 適量的休閒和娛樂 the right amount of leisure and entertainment

→ 培養嗜好 cultivate hobbies

→ 從事體育運動 engage in sports

→ 偶爾離開一陣子 get away once in a while

→ 去度假 go on a vacation

**重點提示**

‧ 不管你是學生或上班族，這都是很容易發揮的題目，你可以分享自己面對的壓力來源，還有自己消除壓力的方法。不過，例文的第一段選擇用第三者的角度，談論學生和上班族共同的兩項壓力來源：實現別人的期望、很難達到理想的生活。

- 由於字數和時間的限制，例文並沒有提到人際關係問題這一點。如果要談這一點的話，可以說因為我們花很多時間和同事在一起（spend a lot of time with our colleagues），所以如果我們不能和他們好好相處（get along with them），會感覺沮喪（feel depressed）、不能把工作做到最好（can't do our best work）。

- 關於消除壓力的方式，大部分的人會想到度假、做運動、享受美食等等，但如果只是把這些方法一項一項列出來，就顯得沒有深度。雖然第二段也提到這種物質性的方式，但把重點放在面對壓力的心態上，主張我們應該學著接受失敗與挫折。

- 雖然題目並沒有要求，但在第一段也稍微提到壓力的正面效果（激勵自己），而壓力之所以有害是因為壓力太重的關係。文章最後的總結也延續這一點，強調除了消除壓力以外，更重要的是將壓力化為正面的力量。只要不離題，而且文意連貫的話，稍微提到與主題相關的其他層面，可以增加內容的豐富度，甚至提升文章視野的高度。

### 作文範例

　　Both students and working adults today are under ①a great deal of stress from the demands of daily life. ②In my opinion, living up to expectations is a main source of stress. ③The fear of disappointing others ④puts enormous pressure on us. Such stress can sometimes motivate us to be academically or professionally successful, but too much of it ⑤can be detrimental to our mental health. ⑥Another source of stress is the difficulty of achieving an ideal lifestyle. The desire to own a house, a car, or luxury goods can be stressful, especially for those who are struggling to ⑦make ends meet.

　　⑧The best way to reduce stress is to develop a positive ⑨mindset. Accept failures as part of life, take responsibility, and learn from our mistakes. ⑩Setting aside some time for recreation also helps to ⑪relieve stress. You can ⑫get involved in sports, take up a new hobby, or get away on vacation ⑬once in a while. ⑭To sum up, there is nothing to fear about stress if we know how to cope with it and turn it into productive energy.

　　今日的學生和有工作的成人，都因為日常生活的要求而壓力很大。就我的看法，實現（別人的）期待是壓力的一個主要來源。害怕讓別人失望的恐懼，帶給我們很大的壓力。這樣的壓力有時能夠激勵我們在學業或職業方面成功，但太多的壓力可能對我們的心理健康有害。另一個壓力的來源是達到理想生活方式的困難。想要擁有房屋、車子或奢侈品的渴望，可能是讓人有壓力的，對於難以收支平衡的人而言尤其如此。

　　減少壓力的最佳方式是培養正面的心態。要接受失敗是生命的一部分、要負責，也要從我們的錯誤中學習。撥出一些時間進行休閒娛樂也有助於緩解壓力。你可以做體育運動、培養新的嗜好，或者偶爾離開度個假。總而言之，如果我們知道如何處理壓力，並且將它轉化為有生產性的能量，那壓力就沒什麼好怕的。

## 文法分析與替換表達方式

① a great deal of（大量的…）。注意後面只能接不可數名詞，例如 time、effort、concentration（專注）等等。

② In my opinion（就我的看法）。這邊也可以換一個角度，用 Based on my personal experience, ...（根據我的個人經驗…），表示是因為自己的實際體會才這樣說。

③ The fear of ...（怕會發生…的恐懼），介系詞 of 後面接可能發生的事情，用名詞或動名詞表示。這個句子的主詞是 fear（不可數名詞），所以主要動詞 put 使用單數形態。

④ put enormous pressure on us 帶給我們很大的壓力
　≒ place considerable pressure on us
　pressure 的語感是「好像壓著人一樣的壓力」，所以傾向用 put、place、exert 等動詞表示「施加／帶來壓力」，不太會說成「bring pressure」。

⑤ can be detrimental to our mental health 可能對我們的心理健康有害
　≒ can have adverse effects on our well-being
　　可能對我們的身心健康有負面影響

detrimental 表示「有害的」。well-being 表示身體、心理等各方面的健康、幸福。

⑥ 這裡用 Another source of stress is... 介紹另一個壓力的來源。或者，也可以說 Stress can also come/stem from...。

⑦ make ends meet（使收支平衡，讓收入足以應付支出）。通常是用在經濟狀況不好、勉強維持生活的情況。關於這個慣用語的來源，有很多種推測，其中一種認為「ends」是表示帳簿上的收入與支出兩邊，所以 make ends meet 就是讓收入和支出能夠相符。

⑧ 主詞是 the way to reduce stress，be 動詞後面接主詞補語，補語部分的 to 不定詞 to develop... 有名詞的功能，而且呼應前面的 to 不定詞結構。不過，也有些特定句型的補語經常會省略不定詞的 to，例如「What you need to do / All you need to do is (to) press this button.」，雖然以傳統的角度來看並不符合文法（主詞的補語應該是名詞或形容詞），但因為現代人的廣泛使用，所以已經成為一般人都接受的用法了。

⑨ mindset（心態）≒ mentality。這裡也可以用 develop a positive perspective（觀點）來表達類似的意思。

⑩ set aside（撥出）≒ put aside，字面上的意思是「放在一邊」，引申為「儲備、預留」。例如：「set aside some money for a rainy day（預留金錢以備困難時使用〔rainy day 比喻遇到困難或窮困的情況〕）」、「set aside some time to relax（撥出一些時間放鬆）」。

⑪ 關於 stress 的一些慣用說法：
reduce stress 減少壓力
relieve stress 紓緩壓力
take away some stress 帶走一些壓力
cope with / deal with / handle stress 處理壓力

⑫ 一些表達「參與、參加」的說法：
get involved in 涉入…，參與…
engage in 從事…
take part in 參加…
participate in 參加…

⑬ once in a while（偶爾）≒ occasionally。依照你想表達的內容，這個句子裡的 once in a while 也可以換成 on a regular basis（定期地）、if the need arises（如果有需要的話）、whenever you like（在任何你想要的時候）等意義不同的說法。

⑭ 一些可以帶出結論的表達方式：

To sum up 總而言之

In conclusion 總之，最後

All in all 考慮到各方面，總而言之

In short 簡而言之

# 複試 口說測驗 解析

▶▶▶ 第一部分 回答問題

你會聽到 8 個問題。每個問題會唸一次。請在聽到題目後立刻回答。第 1 到第 4 題,每題有 15 秒可以回答。第 5 到第 8 題,每題有 30 秒可以回答。

1　Do you enjoy teamwork, or do you prefer to work alone? Please explain your choice.

你喜歡團隊合作,還是偏好獨自工作?請說明你的選擇。

1. 從個人的角度來看,喜歡團隊合作的人可能是因為喜歡和人溝通,而不喜歡的人可能是因為不希望被人打擾。因為題目是問考生自己的偏好,所以不需要很客觀地分析,照自己的想法說明理由就行了。
2. 當然,如果有時間的話,也可以分析一下團隊合作的利弊,例如提高生產力(increase productivity)、促進溝通(improve communication)、花太多時間做決定(take too much time making decisions)、製造衝突(create conflicts)等等。

回答範例 A

I like teamwork. When I'm faced with problems that I can't solve myself, I can ask other team members for help. Even when there is an argument, it's a chance for us to exchange ideas.

我喜歡團隊合作。當我面臨自己不能解決的問題時,我可以向其他團隊成員尋求協助。就算有爭執的時候,也是我們交換意見的機會。

157

When the work isn't complicated, I prefer to do it alone. I don't like it when someone interrupts me, trying to teach me how I should do my job. I'm more efficient when working independently.

當工作不複雜的時候，我偏好自己做。我不喜歡有人打擾我，試圖教我應該怎麼做工作。我獨立作業的時候比較有效率。

單字片語| **teamwork** [ˋtimˋwɝk] n. 團隊合作 / **be faced with** 面臨… / **exchange ideas** 交換意見

---

2 **Have you ever tried to bake a cake yourself? Tell me about your experience.**
你曾經試過自己烤蛋糕嗎？告訴我你的經驗。

**答題策略**

1. 如果烤過蛋糕，那麼包括學做蛋糕的原因、做蛋糕的方法、當時的心情、成功或失敗都是可以談的內容。如果沒做過蛋糕，但做過麵包、餅乾等西式烘焙點心，也可以談談。不過，如果是做饅頭、餃子或者煮菜之類的經驗，就離題太遠了，可能會被認為沒有正確了解題意。
2. 沒有經驗的人，除了談別人做蛋糕的經驗以外，也可以說自己為什麼沒做過或不想做，例如感覺很困難（difficult/challenging）、太花時間（time-consuming），或者沒有一個好的烤箱之類的。

回答範例 A

Yes, and I remember my first baking experience. I found my mom's recipe book and went through the steps of making a sponge cake. It was time-consuming, but fortunately, it turned out to be a success.

是的，而且我記得第一次烘焙的經驗。我發現了媽媽的食譜書，並且照著做海綿蛋糕的步驟做。那很花時間，但幸運的是，結果成功了。

回答範例 B

No, actually I'm such a terrible cook, so I'm afraid I'll mess it up. Besides, it takes a lot of time to prepare ingredients and clean up. It's much easier to buy a delicious cake and enjoy it.

沒有，事實上我很不會烹飪，所以我怕我會搞砸。而且，準備材料和清理會花很多時間。買個美味的蛋糕來享用簡單多了。

單字片語| recipe book 食譜書（烘焙以外的烹飪書可稱為 cookbook） / sponge cake 海綿蛋糕 / time-consuming [ˈtaɪmkənˌsjumɪŋ] adj. 費時的

3 **Your coworkers invite you to join them for dinner, but you have other commitments. Turn them down politely.**

同事邀請你跟他們一起吃晚餐，但你有其他要做的事。禮貌地拒絕他們。

答題策略

題目已經說是因為有其他事情要做，所以在拒絕對方的時候，一定要說明自己是為了做什麼而不能去聚餐。你可以說是因為跟別人約好要做什麼事，或者說跟牙醫有約（I have an appointment with my dentist）、安排了做身體檢查（I'm scheduled for a medical checkup）。

回答範例 A

Next Sunday night? I'd like to join you, but I'm so sorry. It happens to be my wife's birthday, and I promised to take her out for dinner. You guys go ahead and have a good time.

下週日晚上嗎？我很想跟你們一起，但很抱歉。那天剛好是我太太生日，我答應要帶她出門吃晚餐。你們去吧，祝你們過得愉快。

I'm afraid I have to take a rain check. There's some work I have to finish today, or I'll miss the deadline. Next week, I think I can make it then. I'll pay for the drinks.

恐怕我得改天了。我有工作要在今天完成,不然我就趕不上期限了。我想下禮拜我就能到場了。我會付飲料錢。

|單字片語| have other commitments 有其他必須做的事 / happen to do 碰巧… / take a rain check (on...) 改天再接受邀約 / miss a deadline 沒趕上期限

---

**4** **Your aunt wants to invest her life savings into the stock market because her friends are making money. Tell her what you think about it.**

你阿姨想把她的畢生積蓄投資在股市裡,因為她的朋友很賺錢。告訴她你對這件事的想法。

答題策略

1. 關鍵字為 life savings(畢生積蓄),阿姨有點玩太大。你可以用問題來反問她。例如「你對股市了解多少」(How much do you know about the stock market?)、「你知道有什麼風險嗎」(Do you know the risks?)。最後可以建議阿姨不要一次就把所有積蓄投入股市。
2. 你也可以說曾經有人賠很多錢,所以阿姨應該小心謹慎。

回答範例 A

That's a hasty decision. I mean, how much do you know about the stock market? Did you do any research on the companies you want to invest in? I suggest that you talk to a financial planner.

那是很倉促的決定。我的意思是,你對股市了解多少?你研究過你想投資的公司嗎?我建議你跟理財規劃師談。

回答範例 B

I know everyone else is making money, and you're tempted. If I were you, I would invest a small portion instead of all my savings. As the saying goes, "Never put all your eggs in one basket."

我知道別人都賺到錢，所以你很心動。如果我是你的話，我會投資一小部分，而不是所有積蓄。俗話説：「不要把雞蛋都放在同一個籃子裡。」

|單字片語| life savings 畢生積蓄 / stock market 股市 / hasty [`hestɪ] adj. 匆忙的，倉促的 / financial planner 理財規劃師 / tempted [`tɛmptɪd] adj. 受到誘惑的，(tempted to do) 很想做某事的 / As the saying goes, 俗話説…

## 5 Why do you think some people would wait in long lines at famous restaurants?
你覺得為什麼有些人會在知名餐廳排很長的隊？

**答題策略**

在某些餐廳外的確會看到這樣的景象，有可能就是因為餐廳很有名，或者是朋友推薦（because of their friends' recommendation）、被廣告吸引（because they are attracted by the ads）等等。在說明理由之餘，可以說說自己的想法：如果是你的話，願意排隊等候嗎？食物和服務是否值得等待？（Are the food and service worth the wait?）也可以說自己曾經為了等座位而等多久。

回答範例 A

Actually, I'm pretty puzzled. It makes no sense to wait for so long just to eat. I'm the kind of person who hates to wait when I'm hungry. I bet these people must have a lot of time on their hands. Perhaps they were attracted by TV commercials or advertisements. Well, I might do that if the restaurant is offering a special discount.

其實我蠻困惑的。只為了吃東西等這麼久沒有意義。我是那種肚子餓的時候討厭等的人。我敢説這些人一定是時間太多。或許他們是被電視廣告或平面廣告吸引。嗯，如

果那間餐廳有特別折扣的話，我可能會排隊。

B

People like to take pictures of the food in restaurants. With the gaining popularity of social apps such as Facebook, Line, and Instagram, it's much easier for people to share pictures with one another. That's how word of mouth spreads. People would wait in long lines to taste the food their friends recommend.

人們喜歡拍餐廳食物的照片。隨著 Facebook、Line、Instagram 之類的社交 app 越來越流行，彼此分享照片變得容易許多。那就是口碑傳播的方式。人們會排很長的隊去品嚐朋友推薦的食物。

|單字片語| **wait in line** 排隊等候 / **puzzled** [pʌzld] adj. 困惑的 / **make sense** 有意義 / **have time on one's hands** 手頭上有時間→閒著沒事幹 / **gaining popularity** 越來越普及、流行的情況 / **word of mouth** 口碑

6　If you were considering moving to a new place with your six-year-old child, what kind of surrounding do you think is ideal?

如果你在考慮和自己六歲的小孩搬新家，你認為怎樣的周遭環境是理想的？

**答題策略**

如果你未婚也沒有孩子，還是可以做一些假設。例如從別人的情況來想像，如果是你的親戚有六歲小孩呢？要考量的不外乎環境安全，附近還要有小學、公園、圖書館等等。你也可以說自己還是個學生，要回答這個題目有點困難，但你的叔叔有類似的經驗，他理想中的住家環境又是什麼樣子。

A

If I had a six-year-old child, living near schools would be my top priority. Not just any school, but an ideal preschool and elementary school within walking distance. A public library would be a plus. I think a park would also be nice because we can have a picnic there on family days. There should also be supermarkets and convenience stores nearby.

如果我有六歲大的小孩，住在學校附近會是我的第一優先。不是任何學校，而是走路可以到的理想幼稚園和小學。公共圖書館會是額外的有利因素。我認為公園也很棒，因為家庭日的時候我們可以在那裡野餐。附近也應該要有超市和便利商店。

**回答範例 B**

If I had a six-year-old child, safety would be a major concern. The place shouldn't be on a street with heavy traffic. Heavy traffic also causes air and noise pollution. A quiet surrounding would be ideal. It shouldn't be too far away from the school my child would attend. A clinic in the neighborhood would be nice since children get sick easily.

如果我有六歲大的小孩，安全會是我主要關心的。這個地方（新家）不應該在交通繁忙的街道上。繁忙的交通也會造成空氣和噪音污染。安靜的周遭環境會是理想的。這個地方不應該離我小孩上的學校太遠。附近有診所會很棒，因為小孩很容易生病。

|單字片語| **surrounding** [sə`raʊndɪŋ] n. 周遭環境 / **top priority** 第一優先 / **preschool** [`pri`skul] n. 幼稚園 / **within walking distance** 在走路可以到的距離內

7 **What are the advantages and disadvantages of sending young children to bilingual schools?**
送孩童去上雙語學校有什麼優點和缺點？

**答題策略**

雙語學校的英文課肯定比一般學校多。有些人覺得學習應該從小開始，特別是語言。不過也有些人覺得應該先把中文學好才開始學外語。另外，雙語學

校的收費並不便宜，所以或許有足夠的錢才能考慮雙語學校。除了學校本身以外，也可以說如果用網路上的免費資源（use free resources on the Internet），就不一定要花大錢。

The main advantage is the number of hours of English lessons. When it comes to learning a language, the younger, the better. Most bilingual schools employ native speakers from America and Canada. Children will learn to speak English with the right accent from an early age. The only disadvantage I can think of is the tuition fee.

主要的優點是英語課的時數。說到學習語言，年紀越小越好。大部分雙語學校雇用來自美國和加拿大的母語人士。小孩會從很小的年紀就學習用正確的腔調說英語。我能想到的唯一缺點是學費。

In my opinion, bilingual schools can be quite stressful for kids. For young children, learning both Chinese and English at the same time is confusing. I think they should be proficient in their mother tongue before being exposed to a second language. That said, I have to admit that some children are capable of speaking fluently in two languages if they learn at a young age.

就我看來，雙語學校對小孩而言可能很有壓力。對年幼的小孩來說，同時學習中英文是很讓人困惑的。我想他們在接觸第二語言之前應該先熟練母語。話雖如此，我必須承認有些小孩如果在很小的時候開始學，就能夠把兩種語言說得很流利。

|單字片語| bilingual [baɪˋlɪŋgwəl] adj. 雙語的 / employ [ɪmˋplɔɪ] v. 雇用 / native speaker 母語人士 / accent [ˋæksɛnt] n. 口音，腔調 / from an early age 從年紀很小的時候開始 / tuition fee 學費 / stressful [ˋstrɛsfəl] adj. 壓力大的 / proficient [prəˋfɪʃənt] adj. 精通的，熟練的 / mother tongue 母語 / be exposed to 暴露於⋯ / That (being) said, 話雖如此⋯ / be capable of doing 有能力做⋯

## 8  Do you think starting salary matters the most when it comes to finding a job? Please explain.

你認為找工作時起薪最重要嗎？請說明。

### 答題策略

起薪越高，也會有比較高的加薪（pay raise）和年終獎金（year-end bonus）。因為物價上漲（rising prices），所以或許薪水高是最實際的。不過，也有人認為第一份工作的起薪不重要，重要的是先有工作，得到經驗後再要求更高的薪資或找別的工作。

### 回答範例 A

I agree that starting salary matters a lot. Even a difference of two or three thousand dollars per month is rather significant. Add that up, and it turns out to be a big sum of money in a year. With inflation and rising prices, it is important that we start our careers with a slightly higher salary. Starting salary also affects the pay raise and annual bonus we get in the future.

我同意起薪非常重要。即使每月兩、三千元的差距也相當重要。把它加起來，一年後就會累積成很大的金額。因為通貨膨脹、物價上漲，所以我們用高一點的薪水開始就職是很重要的。起薪也會影響我們未來獲得的加薪和年終獎金。

### 回答範例 B

I don't think starting salary is the most important thing. As long as we like the job, we can start low and work our way up. By working hard and proving our worth, sooner or later we'll get a raise. Many rich and famous people started their careers with humble pay. Furthermore, the first job we get could be just a stepping stone.

我認為起薪不是最重要的。只要我們喜歡這份工作，我們可以從低處開始，然後努力往上爬。靠著努力工作和證明自己的價值，我們遲早會獲得加薪。許多有錢、有名的人剛開始工作時薪水很微薄。而且，我們得到的第一份工作可能只是一塊跳板。

▶▶▶ 第二部分 **看圖敘述**

> 請看照片，用 30 秒的時間思考以下問題，然後用 1 分半的時間錄下你的回答。

1. Where was this picture probably taken? What makes you think so?
2. What are the people doing? Have you ever been in a similar situation? Tell me about your experience.
3. What may be the reason that the vehicle on the left side of the road is adopted in this place?
4. Do you think this kind of vehicle is ideal for your hometown? Please explain.
5. If you still have time, please describe the picture in as much detail as you can.

1. 這張照片可能是在哪裡拍的？為什麼你這麼認為？
2. 這些人在做什麼？你曾經處在類似的情況嗎？告訴我你的經驗。
3. 道路左邊的運輸工具在這裡獲得採用的理由可能是什麼？
4. 你認為這種運輸工具適合你的家鄉嗎？請說明。
5. 如果你還有時間，請盡量詳細描述這張照片。

## 草稿擬定

1. 先從圖中的建築物猜測拍攝地點
2. 從路面電車進一步確定所在地
3. 針對等待路面電車的人群做出觀察
4. 特別提到站在前面拍照的人
5. 說明路面電車的優點（除了範例中提到的 streetcar、tram 等名稱，也可以說是 light rail train〔輕軌列車〕；真的想不到任何名稱的話，也可以說這是一種「public transportation」或「electric train」）

## 加分延伸

對於台灣是否適合路面電車的問題，可以提到它有減少空氣污染、比地下鐵低的建設費用（construction cost）等優點。不過，道路安全（road safety）是個問題，很難預防和汽車的衝撞（collision），所以也需要有新的交通法規（traffic laws）。

### 回答範例

There are many people in the picture, who are standing in line at a bus stop. Allow me to correct myself, I mean a streetcar stop. They're waiting for the streetcar. I see the rails in the ground now. A streetcar is an excellent form of public transportation. In fact, streetcars are far better than buses. They produce less air and noise pollution. A friend of mine mentioned once that sitting on a streetcar is more comfortable than sitting on a bus. Streetcars are more common in European countries, so I guess this picture must be taken in a European city. The buildings and even street lights are very different from those in Asian countries. I wish I grew up in such a lovely and romantic place. I plan to visit London this summer, so I'm looking forward to taking a streetcar. Oh, it's called "tram" there. By the way, I notice a woman who is taking a picture of the approaching streetcar. I bet she must be a tourist. Locals who take it daily are unlikely to take a picture of something they see so often. To be honest, I'm not sure if streetcars will work in Taiwan. Cars and pedestrians have to get out of the way and not obstruct streetcars from moving forward. In addition, people should refrain from littering because trash may get stuck in the rails and cause accidents. Given the fact that there are so many scooter riders in Taiwan, streetcars could pose a problem.

範例中譯

照片裡有許多人，他們站在公車站排隊。讓我修正一下，我是說路面電車站。他們在等路面電車。我現在看到地上的軌道了。路面電車是很好的大眾運輸形式。事實上，路面電車比公車好多了。它們產生的空氣污染和噪音污染比較少。我有個朋友曾經提到，坐在路面電車上比坐在公車上舒服。路面電車在歐洲國家比較普遍，所以我猜這張照片一定是在歐洲城市拍的。這些建築物，甚至是路燈，都和亞洲國家非常不同。我希望我在這麼可愛又浪漫的地方長大。我打算今年夏天拜訪倫敦，所以我很期待搭路面電車。噢，在那裡叫「tram」。對了，我注意到有個女的在拍進站中的路面電車。我敢說她一定是觀光客。每天搭的當地人不太可能會拍很常看到的東西。老實說，我不確定路面電車在台灣行得通。車輛和行人必須讓路，不要阻擋路面電車前進。而且，人們應該不要亂丟垃圾，因為垃圾可能會被卡在軌道上，並且造成意外。考慮到台灣有這麼多機車騎士的事實，路面電車可能造成問題。

|單字片語| **streetcar** [ˋstritˌkɑr] n. 路面電車，輕軌電車（美、加用語，英國稱為 **tram** [træm]）/ **rail** [rel] n. 鐵軌 / **public transportation** 大眾運輸（工具）/ **street light** 路燈 / **local** [ˋlokl] n. 當地人 / **obstruct** [əbˋstrʌkt] v. 阻擋 / **refrain from doing** 忍住不做⋯，避免做⋯ / **litter** [ˋlɪtɚ] n. 亂丟垃圾

▶▶▶ 第三部分 **申述**

請用 1 分半的時間思考你對於以下問題的答案，然後用 1 分半的時間錄下你的回答。你可以用測驗卷做筆記並整理你的想法。

Electric cars are getting more and more popular these years. What are some benefits of electric cars, and what should be improved to make them more appealing to people? Please explain.

電動車在這幾年越來越流行。電動車的一些好處是什麼，又應該改進什麼來讓它們更吸引人？請說明。

第 1 回
第 2 回
第 3 回
第 4 回
第 5 回
第 6 回

### 草稿擬定

1. 電動車的好處：環保、安靜、性能佳
2. 電動車需要改進的地方：充電不方便（當然，價格太貴也是可以提到的一點）
3. 缺點改善後，電動車會更加流行

### 加分延伸

如果你平常注意時事，可以提到台灣政府計畫在 2040 年禁止銷售所有使用化石燃料的汽車（ban the sale of fossil-fuel cars from 2040），其他許多國家也有類似的政策，所以各大車廠都努力投入電動車的開發。

### 回答範例

Electric cars have several benefits. First, it's obvious that they are friendlier to the environment. Unlike fossil-fuel cars, electric cars don't emit exhaust fumes, so they can help improve air quality in urban areas. Electric cars also emit less greenhouse gases, such as carbon dioxide, so they're also a good solution to fight climate change. Second, electric cars are far more silent than traditional cars. Since they're not powered by combustion engines, the only noises they make are caused by their tires or by wind resistance. Therefore, their drivers can better enjoy music without turning up the volume too much. Last but not least, it is easier to drive an electric car. There's no need to change gears, yet it can accelerate faster than a gas-powered car. Therefore, it can easily climb on steep slopes with maximum

169

power. Also, electric car drivers find that they don't need to use the brake pedal, as the car can immediately slow down when they lift off the accelerator pedal. In short, electric cars not only benefit the environment, but also provide better driving experience. However, charging is still a significant problem. At normal charging stations, it takes hours to fully charge the battery, so it's better to install charging equipment at home and charge at night. Unfortunately, most apartment buildings in Taiwan don't allow their residents to do so. If there are more charging stations that charge faster, I believe more people will be convinced to buy electric cars.

### 範例中譯

電動車有幾項好處。首先，電動車顯然比較環保。不像化石燃料的車輛，電動車不會排放廢氣，所以能幫助改善都市地區的空氣品質。電動車排放的溫室氣體也比較少，例如二氧化碳，所以也是對抗氣候變遷的好辦法。第二，電動車遠比傳統車安靜。因為它們不是由燃油引擎推動，所以它們製造的噪音就只是輪胎或風阻產生的。所以，電動車駕駛更能享受音樂，而不用把音量調得太高。最後同樣重要的是，開電動車比較簡單。（開電動車）不需要換檔，但電動車加速卻能比汽油動力車快。所以，電動車能輕易用最大馬力爬上陡峭的斜坡。而且，電動車駕駛人發現他們不需要使用煞車踏板，因為當他們鬆開加速踏板的時候，車子可以馬上慢下來。簡而言之，電動車不止對環境有益，也提供比較好的駕駛體驗。不過，充電仍然是個顯著的問題。在一般的充電站，充滿電池要花很長的時間，所以在家安裝充電設備並且在晚上充電是比較好的。遺憾的是，台灣大部分的公寓大樓不允許居民這麼做。如果有更多充電比較快的充電站，我相信更多人會被說服買電動車。

|單字片語| **fossil fuel** 化石燃料 / **exhaust fumes** 引擎排放的廢氣 / **emit** [ɪˋmɪt] v. 散發，排出 / **greenhouse gas** 溫室氣體 / **dioxide** [daɪˋɑksaɪd] n. 二氧化物 / **climate change** 氣候變遷 / **combustion engine** 以燃料推動的引擎 / **wind resistance** 風阻 / **change gears** （開車時）換檔 / **accelerate** [ækˋsɛləˌret] v. 加速 / **accelerator** [ækˋsɛləˌretɚ] n. 加速裝置

# 第六回　寫作能力測驗答題注意事項

1. 本測驗共有兩部分。第一部分為中譯英，第二部分為引導寫作。測驗時間為 **50 分鐘**。

2. 請利用試題紙空白處及背面擬稿，但正答務必書寫在「寫作能力測驗答案紙」上。在答案紙以外的地方作答，不予計分。

3. 第一部分中譯英請在答案紙第一頁開始作答，第二部分引導寫作請自答案紙第二頁起作答。

4. 作答時請勿隔行書寫，請注意字跡應清晰可讀，並請保持答案紙之清潔，以免影響評分。

5. 未獲監試人員指示前，請勿翻閱試卷。

6. 測驗時，不得在考試通知或其他物品上抄題，亦不得有傳遞、夾帶小抄、左顧右盼或交談等違規行為。

7. 意圖或已經將試卷攜出試場者，五年內不得報名參加本測驗。請人代考者，連同代考者，三年內不得報名參加本測驗。

8. 測驗結束時，須立即停止作答，在原位靜候監試人員收回全部試卷及答案紙，清點無誤後，宣佈結束始可離場。

9. 應試者入場、出場及測驗中如有違反上列規則或不服監試人員之指示者，監試人員得取消其應試資格並請其離場，且作答不予計分。

# 全民英語能力分級檢定測驗
## GENERAL ENGLISH PROFICIENCY TEST
## High-Intermediate Level Writing Test

### Part I: Chinese-English Translation (40%)

Translate the following Chinese passage into an English passage, and write your answer on the Writing Test Answer Sheet.

台灣許多大學正感受到低出生率的衝擊。隨著學生人口的減少，比較不受歡迎的大學可能發現很難吸引優秀的學生。事實上，大學名額數已經超過了畢業高中生人數。有些學校催促政府允許更多中國學生在台灣接受教育。為了生存，大學招募來自東南亞的學生並不少見，有的甚至選擇合併。

### Part II: Guided Writing (60%)

Write an essay of **150~180 words** in an appropriate style on the following topic. Write your answer on the Writing Test Answer Sheet.

Whether social media companies have the right to ban certain users has sparked a heated debate. Some argue that social media companies have the public responsibility to silence those who spread false information and hate speech, while others think the companies may have too much power over the speech of their users. In your essay, you should
(1) analyze reasons for and against banning someone from social media, and
(2) express your attitude toward the issue.

# 全民英語能力檢定測驗
## 中高級寫作能力測驗答案紙

第一部分請由第 1 行開始作答，勿隔行書寫。第二部分請翻至第 2 頁作答。

1 _____

_____

_____

_____

5 _____

_____

_____

_____

_____

10_____

_____

_____

_____

_____

15_____

第二部分請翻至第 2 頁作答。

1

5

10

15

20

25

30

35

40

45

50

55

60

# 第六回　口說能力測驗答題注意事項

1. 本測驗問題由耳機播放，回答則經麥克風錄下。分回答問題、看圖敘述與申述題三部份，時間共約 20 分鐘，連同口試說明時間共需約 50 分鐘。

2. 第一部份回答問題的題目只播出一次，聽完題目後請立即回答。第二部份看圖敘述有 30 秒的思考時間及 1 分 30 秒的答題時間；第三部份申述題分別有 1 分 30 秒的思考時間及答題時間。思考時，請不要發出聲音。等聽到指示開始回答時，請針對圖片或申述題的題目在作答時間內盡量的表達。

3. 錄音設備皆已事先完成設定，請勿觸動任何機件，以免影響錄音。測驗時請戴妥耳機，將麥克風調到嘴邊約三公分處，依指示以適中音量回答。

4. 測驗進行間，不可以在試題紙以外任何物品上書寫與測驗相關之任何文字、符號，亦不可有傳遞、夾帶小抄、左顧右盼或交談等違規行為，否則作答不予計分。

5. 意圖或已將試題紙或試題影音資料攜出或傳送出試場者，視同侵犯本中心著作財產權，限五年內不得報名參加「全民英檢」測驗。請人代考者，連同代考者，三年內不得報名參加本測驗。

6. 測驗結束時，須立即停止作答，在原位靜候監試人員收回全部試題紙並清點無誤，等候監試人員宣布結束後始可離場。

7. 入場、出場及測驗中如有違反上列規則或不服監試人員之指示者，監試人員將取消您的應試資格並請您離場，且測驗成績不予計分，亦不退費。

# 全民英語能力分級檢定測驗
## GENERAL ENGLISH PROFICIENCY TEST

## High-Intermediate Level Speaking Test

**Please read the self-introduction sentence.**

My seat number is (座位號碼後 5 碼) , and my registration number is (考試號碼後 5 碼) .

## Part 1　Answering Questions

You will hear 8 questions. Each question will be spoken once. Please answer the question immediately after you hear it.

For questions 1 to 4, you will have 15 seconds to answer each question.

For questions 5 to 8, you will have 30 seconds to answer each question.

**Part II   Picture Description**

Look at the picture, think about the questions below for 30 seconds, and then record your answers for 1½ minutes.

1. Where was this picture probably taken? What makes you think so?
2. What are the people at the bottom of the picture doing? Have you ever seen such a scene in person or on the media? Tell me about your experience.
3. Why is this kind of action popular in similar occasions?
4. Do you think you would enjoy a night at such an occasion? Please explain.
5. If you still have time, please describe the picture in as much detail as you can.

## Part III    Discussion

Think about your answer(s) to the question(s) below for 1½ minutes, and then record your answer(s) for 1½ minutes. You may use your test paper to make notes and organize your ideas.

What may be the reasons that drunk driving increases the risk of fatal car accidents? What can be done to prevent people from drinking and driving? Please explain.

**Please read the self-introduction sentence again.**

My seat number is (座位號碼後 5 碼) , and my registration number is (考試號碼後 5 碼) .

## 複試 寫作測驗 解析

▶▶▶ 　　　　　中譯英 (40%)

將以下這段中文翻譯成英文。

台灣許多大學正感受到低出生率的衝擊。隨著學生人口的減少,比較不受歡迎的大學可能發現很難吸引優秀的學生。事實上,大學名額數已經超過了畢業高中生人數。有些學校催促政府允許更多中國學生在台灣接受教育。為了生存,大學招募來自東南亞的學生並不少見,有的甚至選擇合併。

Many universities in Taiwan are feeling the impact of a low birth rate. With the decline in student population, universities that are less popular may find it hard to attract outstanding students. In fact, the number of university places has already exceeded that of graduating high school students. Some schools urge the government to allow more students from China to receive education in Taiwan. In order to survive, it is not uncommon for universities to recruit students from Southeast Asia, and some even choose to merge.

### 逐句說明

**1. 台灣許多大學正感受到低出生率的衝擊。**

Many universities in Taiwan are feeling the impact of a low birth rate.

• 「衝擊」:impact。有幾個單字可以表達「影響」的意思,例如 impact、influence、effect 等等,但用法有些不同。effect 除了「影響」以外,還能表示「效果」、「效應」,例如藥的效果、酒精對人的影響作用等等。influence 經常用來表示抽象的、心理或權力方面的「影響

181

力」，例如網路對現代人生活的影響、某個人或某本書對我們的想法、行為的影響。impact 的原意是「衝擊、撞擊」，和中文翻譯的語感差不多，表示非常大的影響。這裡的中文已經給了「衝擊」這個提示，低出生率也的確會帶來很大的影響，所以 impact 是最適合的翻譯。

- 「出生率」：birth rate。其他關於社會統計的「率」還有：divorce rate（離婚率）、unemployment rate（失業率）、crime rate（犯罪率）等等。

## 2. 隨著學生人口的減少，比較不受歡迎的大學可能發現很難吸引優秀的學生。

With the decline in student population, universities that are less popular may find it hard to attract outstanding students.

- 「隨著…的減少」：With the decline in...。雖然「減少」直接翻譯成英文會是 decrease，但比較少看到「With the decrease in...」這種說法（不過，With the increase 則很常用），所以這裡使用 decline（下降，減少）。或者，這裡也可以換一個句型，把 decrease 當成動詞使用就可以了：As the student population decreases, ...。

- 「比較不受歡迎的」：less popular。如果能先想到「受歡迎的」是 popular，這部分的翻譯就一點也不難了。可能有人會翻成 more unpopular，但語感比較像是「已經有些大學很不受歡迎，而這些大學還更糟糕」，負面意味比較強，但中文純粹是表達單純的比較關係，所以翻成 more unpopular 比較不貼切。

- 表示一間學校的優點，除了 popular（受歡迎）以外，還有可能使用這些形容詞：well-known（知名的）、reputable（聲譽好的）、prestigious（有名望的）。

## 3. 事實上，大學名額數已經超過了畢業高中生人數。

In fact, the number of university places has already exceeded that of graduating high school students.

- 「the number of A（複數名詞）」可以理解為「A 的 number」→「A 的數目」，主詞是 number，視為單數，動詞用單數形。至於「a number of

A（複數名詞）」，則是「有若干數目的 A」→「許多 A」，主詞是
A，動詞用複數形。例如：「The number of students is increasing.（學生
人數正在增加）」、「A number of students are from the United States.
（有許多學生來自美國）」。

- 「名額數」：number of places。也可以換個講法，說成 the number of
students demanded by universities（大學要求的學生人數）。

- 因為前面已經出現過 number of...（…的數目），所以後面為了不要重複
number 這個字，必須改用指示代名詞 that；that of graduating high school
students 就是 the number of graduating high school students 的意思。如果
要代替的重複單字是複數的話，就改成 those，例如：「The students in
Taiwan are less independent compared with those in the United States.（比起
美國的學生，台灣的學生沒有那麼獨立）」。

## 4. 有些學校催促政府允許更多中國學生在台灣接受教育。

**Some schools urge the government to allow more students from China to receive education in Taiwan.**

- 「催促／力勸 A 做…」：urge A to do...。或者使用 urge that A do（原形
動詞）的句型，表示「強力主張」或「呼籲」的意思。不管是同等關
係、上對下或下對上的關係，都可以使用 urge 這個字，例如：「Various
corporations urge the government to lower taxes.（多家公司要求政府減
稅）」、「The government urges corporations to raise salaries.（政府要求
公司加薪）」。

## 5. 為了生存，大學招募來自東南亞的學生並不少見，有的甚至選擇合併。

**In order to survive, it is not uncommon for universities to recruit students from Southeast Asia, and some even choose to merge.**

- In order to do... 可以省略成 To do...。

- 「A 做…並不少見」：it is not uncommon for A to do...。或者也可以用「it
is not uncommon that 子句」的句型，寫成：It is not uncommon that
universities recruit students from Southeast Asia。不過，不管怎樣都是把 it

is not uncommon 寫在句子前面，和中文的順序很不一樣，平時應該多注意這種使用虛主詞 it、順序和中文不同的句型。

依照以下主題，以適當的文體寫一篇 150~180 字的短文。

Whether social media companies have the right to ban certain users has sparked a heated debate. Some argue that social media companies have the public responsibility to silence those who spread false information and hate speech, while others think the companies may have too much power over the speech of their users. In your essay, you should
(1) analyze reasons for and against banning someone from social media, and
(2) express your attitude toward the issue.

社交媒體公司是否有權禁止特定用戶，引起了激烈的辯論。有些人主張社交媒體公司有將散播假資訊與仇恨言論的人禁言的公共責任，其他人則認為這些公司可能對用戶的言論擁有太大的權力。在短文中，你應該
(1) 分析支持和反對禁止某人使用社交媒體的理由，並且
(2) 表達你對這個議題的態度。

### 草稿擬定

根據題目的提示，先設想大致上的文章結構，然後列舉自己想到的細節內容。這些內容可能沒辦法全部寫進文章，但可以作為寫作時的參考。

## a. 支持禁止特定用戶使用社交媒體的理由

→ 停止假訊息與仇恨言論的散播
  deter the spread of false information and hate speech

→ 讓人打消故意違反服務條款的念頭
  discourage people from deliberately violating terms of service

第 1 回

第 2 回

第 3 回

第 4 回

第 5 回

第 6 回

→ 仇恨言論可能引起對某些人的暴力行為
hate speech can incite violence against some people

→ 有嚴重偏見的意見實際上會妨礙民主的討論
highly biased opinions actually hinders democratic debate

## b. 反對禁止特定用戶使用社交媒體的理由

→ 社交媒體公司對於決定要禁止誰可能有偏見
social media companies can be biased in deciding who to ban

→ 一個人被禁止的原因並不總是很清楚
it is not always clear why a person is banned

→ 用戶可能被鼓勵自我審查
users may be encouraged to censor themselves

→ 禁止並不會解決問題：被禁止的內容可能出現在其他任何地方
banning does not solve the problem: banned content can appear anywhere else

**重點提示**

• 仔細閱讀題目的說明是很重要的。這一類「二選一／表達態度」的題目，有時候只要求你選擇其中一個看法，但這裡題目的項目 (1) 要求「analyze reasons for AND against…」，所以不能只給贊成的理由或反對的理由，必須兼顧正反雙方。因為篇幅的關係，所以最合理的方法是在第一段或文章前半分別討論支持和反對禁止特定用戶的理由。

• 和前幾回的作文範例一樣，這裡的例文也只選擇了草稿階段想到的部分論點，不必全部寫進文章裡面。

• 題目要求你二選一或表達態度時，除了選邊站以外，也可以考慮是否有其他的可能。以這個題目為例，也可以建議由社交網站之外的獨立機構（independent institution）來管制言論；或者禁言與否並不重要，重要的是人們對於網路上的言論要有獨立思考（independent thinking）的能力。

• 這裡比較困難的是，第一段已經寫了正反雙方的理由，第二段如何進一步發展下去。如果兩段的內容大同小異，一直重複類似論點的話，會因為內容結構不佳而無法獲得高分。例文的第二段同樣提到了支持的理由，但改以個人的實際觀察作為主要的內容。你也可以選擇談論自己看到某些言論時的心理反應，或者舉出社會上實際發生的例子來支持你的選擇（如果你知道事件的來龍去脈的話）。總之，不同的段落應該展現出同一主題的不同層面，才是結構良好的文章。

①Misinformation and hate speech are ②rampant on social media, and leading companies, such as Facebook and Twitter, try to combat such content by banning certain users. Many are in favor of this approach, ③considering that it can effectively ④deter the spread of toxic content and discourage users from deliberately violating rules. It may also prevent the possibility that online hate turns into real-life violence. ⑤On the other hand, some argue that social media companies should not be given control over ⑥free speech, since they can be ⑦biased in deciding who to ⑧suspend, and it is not always clear why a user is suspended.

Personally, even though there are cases of people being banned by mistake, I still believe social media companies should regulate speech. I often see people share fake news and make ⑨ungrounded criticisms, and many would concur with them without ⑩verifying the information. Not everyone can ⑪apply critical thinking to what they see, so I think those who spread misleading information should be suspended immediately.

錯誤訊息和仇恨言論在社交媒體上很猖獗，而 Facebook 和 Twitter 之類的龍頭公司試圖藉由禁止特定用戶來對抗這種內容。許多人支持這個作法，認為能夠有效阻止有害內容的散播，並且讓用戶打消故意違反規定的念頭。這樣可能也會預防網路上的仇恨轉變為實際生活中的暴力行為的可能性。另一方面，有些人主張社交媒體公司不應該得到對於言論自由的控制權，因為它們在決定要停止誰的使用權時可能會有偏見，而且用戶被停止使用權的理由並不是隨時都很清楚。

就我個人而言，雖然有一些被錯誤地禁止使用的例子，我仍然相信社交媒體公司應該管制言論。我常常看到有人分享假新聞並且做出沒有根據的批評，許多人會贊同他們而不查證資訊的真實性。並不是每個人都能對自己看到的東西進行批判性思考，所以我認為散播誤導人的資訊的人應該立刻被停止使用權。

① misinformation（錯誤資訊）≒ false/wrong/inaccurate information。和另一個類似的詞 disinformation（造假資訊）不同，disinformation 是故意捏造、用來欺騙別人的資訊，misinformation 則不一定有這樣的意圖，有可能是連作者自己也信以為真的。所以，可以說 misinformation 的定義範圍比 disinformation 來得大。

② rampant（猖獗的）≒ widespread ≒ prevalent。但要注意 rampant 通常都是用在不好的事物很常見的情況。

③ 這裡的分詞構句，可以理解為省略表示理由的連接詞，也就是 because they (= many [people]) consider... 的意思。

④ deter the spread of toxic content 阻止有害內容的傳播

　　≒ stop toxic content from spreading 阻止有害內容傳播

　　≒ prevent toxic content from being circulated 預防有害內容被流通

⑤ 請記住 On one hand（一方面…）、On the other hand（另一方面…）這兩個片語，經常用在有兩個方面要討論的時候，在文章中分別引導關於這兩方面的內容。這篇文章只使用了 On the other hand，但如果用了 On one hand 的話，通常一定會搭配 On the other hand 來用。

⑥ free speech ≒ freedom of speech。另外，談到言論自由的時候，也常會提到 the First Amendment（美國憲法第一修正案），這項法案禁止美國國會制定妨害言論自由的法律，所以在討論美國政府是否應該介入管制網路言論時，就會討論是否違反了 the First Amendment。

⑦ biased（有偏見的）≒ prejudiced ≒ unfair

⑧ suspend（暫時禁止某人的活動）和 ban 的意思差不多。因為文章裡多次提到「禁止」，為了避免用詞重複，所以在一些地方改用 suspend 這個字，是英文作文很基本的技巧。

⑨ ungrounded（沒有根據的）≒ baseless ≒ unfounded

⑩ verify the information 查證資訊

　　≒ check whether the information is true 檢查資訊是否為真

　　≒ make sure the information is true 確認資訊是真的

⑪ 這裡把 critical thinking（批判性思考）看成一種方法，並且 apply to（用於…）接收到的資訊。也可以用動詞的形式 critically think about 來表達。

學習筆記欄

# 複試 口說測驗 解析

▶▶▶ 回答問題

> 你會聽到 8 個問題。每個問題會唸一次。請在聽到題目後立刻回答。第 1 到第 4 題，每題有 15 秒可以回答。第 5 到第 8 題，每題有 30 秒可以回答。

## 1 Do you feel stressed when you need to give a public speech? Why or why not?

**當你需要公開演說的時候，你會緊張嗎？為什麼？**

 答題策略

1. 一般人需要公開演說時都會害怕，特別是在陌生人面前演講。你可以說你有過的經驗（回答範例 B）。不過，如果你因為工作的關係需要經常發表演講，公開演說對你而言可能就不是問題（回答範例 A）。
2. 如果還有時間，可以說你想要增進自己的公開演說技巧（improve my public speech skills），想上訓練課程（take a training course），或者從網路上的 TED 演講學習（learn from TED talks online）。

回答範例 A

As a matter of fact, I look forward to giving a public speech. As a project manager, I have to speak in front of different groups of people. I find it challenging and exciting.

事實上，我很期待公開演說。身為專案經理，我必須在各種不同的團體面前說話。我覺得這既有挑戰性又刺激。

Public speaking is my worst nightmare. I get cold feet and butterflies in my stomach when I face the audience. I worry about forgetting my lines or saying the wrong things.

公開演說是我最恐怖的惡夢。我面對聽眾就會怯場而且緊張。我擔心忘記自己的台詞或者說錯話。

|單字片語| **project manager** 專案經理（**PM**）/ **nightmare** [ˈnaɪtˌmɛr] n. 惡夢 / **get cold feet** 臨陣退縮，怯場 / **get butterflies in ones' stomach** 緊張

## 2 Have you ever been to a classical music concert? Tell me about your experience.
### 你去過古典音樂會嗎？告訴我你的經驗。

**答題策略**

1. 如果曾經去過，或者在電視上看過，可以描述古典音樂會的場景，還有你覺得精彩的地方。如果沒有這種經驗，可以說你只去過流行歌手或搖滾樂團的演唱會（英文一樣叫 concert），那時候的經驗又是如何。
2. 古典音樂會是個隆重的場合，你可以提到其他人的穿著，還有一些必須遵守的禮儀（etiquette，不可數名詞；或者說是 rules），例如不能大聲講話（talk too loud）、必須等表演結束才鼓掌（applaud only when the performance is complete）。

回答範例 A

My wife and I went to a classical music concert for the first time in our lives last month. It was an eye-opening experience. It was amazing that all those musicians coordinated their actions so well.

上個月，我跟我太太是這輩子第一次去古典音樂會。那是令人大開眼界的經驗。整群樂手的動作協調得這麼好，真的很驚人。

回答範例 B

I'm afraid not. I'm not passionate about classical music. I prefer Taiwanese pop music. I went to Jiang Hui's concert after she announced that she was retiring. It was a memorable experience.

可惜沒有。我對古典音樂並不熱衷。我比較喜歡台語流行音樂。江蕙宣布要退休時，我去了她的演唱會。那是個難忘的經驗。

┃單字片語┃ **classical music** 古典音樂 / **eye-opening** 讓人大開眼界的 / **musician** [mjuˋzɪʃən] n. 音樂家，音樂人，樂手 / **coordinate** [koˋɔrdnet] v. （使）協調 / **passionate** [ˋpæʃənɪt] adj. 熱情的 / **memorable** [ˋmɛmərəbl] adj. 難忘的，值得紀念的

3　**Your friend Sam's parents are considering a divorce. Try to cheer him up.**
你朋友 Sam 的父母正在考慮離婚。試著讓他心情開朗一點。

**答題策略**

你可以勸朋友接受這個事實。跟他說父母離婚並不是他的錯，然後轉移焦點，想辦法讓他開心。告訴他這不是世界末日（the end of the world），盡量往好的方面想。不過，既然題目用的是 considering（正在考慮），表示事情還有轉圜的餘地，你也可以勸朋友設法幫他們重修舊好（try to help them make it up）。

回答範例 A

This is bad news indeed, but there is nothing you can do. It's not your fault. Why don't we go for a drink? My treat. Let's go to a KTV after that and leave our troubles behind.

這真是個壞消息，但你什麼也做不了。這不是你的錯。我們何不去喝一杯呢？我請客。然後我們去 KTV，把煩惱拋在腦後。

Look on the bright side. You're eighteen years old, so they won't have to fight over your custody. Sometimes we can never understand what the adults are thinking. Come on. Let's play basketball.

你要往好處想。你 18 歲,所以他們不必為了你的監護權爭吵。有時候我們永遠沒辦法了解大人在想什麼。來吧。我們打籃球。

|單字片語| **divorce** [dəˋvors] n. v. 離婚 / **go for a drink** 去喝一杯(去喝酒) / **My treat.** 我請客。 / **KTV** 卡拉OK的中式說法(英語系國家通常稱為 karaoke bar) / **leave one's troubles behind** 把煩惱拋在腦後 / **look on the bright side** 看積極的一面,往好處想 / **custody** [ˋkʌstədɪ] n. 監護(權)

## 4 Your uncle will be retiring soon. Tell him what he can do with his free time.
你叔叔很快就要退休了。告訴他空閒時間可以怎麼利用。

**答題策略**

退休人士在空閒時間找點事做,可以避免憂鬱症和老年癡呆症(prevent depression and dementia)。考慮到對方是長輩,所以你的建議不要顯得有威脅性或者沒禮貌。想一些有助於打發時間(kill time)、認識新朋友(meet new friends),又有意義的休閒活動。你也可以建議他當義工,甚至找兼職工作。

回答範例 A

I think you should do some volunteer work either at a hospital or a home for the elderly. Making yourself useful is a good way to kill time. Retirement can bore you to death if you stay idle.

我想你應該在醫院或養老院做義工。讓自己有用是打發時間的好方法。如果你無所事事的話,退休會讓你非常無聊。

回答範例 B

Uncle Sam, why not learn a new language? That will keep you occupied. You always wanted to learn Japanese, didn't you? To live is to learn. You're never too old to learn anything.

Sam 叔叔，何不學新的語言呢？那會讓你有事做。你一直都想學日語不是嗎？活著就是為了學習。學任何事情永遠都不嫌年紀太大。

|單字片語| idle [`aɪdl] adj. 閒散的，無所事事的 / occupied [`ɑkjopaɪd] adj. 忙於某事的

5 Why do many people think it is necessary to buy a home before marriage?

為什麼許多人認為結婚前買房子是必要的？

**答題策略**

1. 買房子或許是為了實際生活方面的考量，例如不用擔心租約到期要搬家，或者是為了生小孩做準備。另外，心理因素也很重要，例如可以帶來安全感（sense of security）、代表擁有和伴侶獨處的地方（回答範例 A）。另外，買房子也可以避免和對方家人（in-laws）同住可能產生的衝突（回答範例 B）。

2. 因為題目問的是「為什麼許多人認為必須買房子」，所以就算你不同意，也必須先討論買房子的理由，有多餘的時間才去談不必買房子的原因，或者你個人的想法。

回答範例 A

I think it's like a symbol of love and commitment. For a married couple, having their own home means they have a private place to concentrate on each other. They may feel insecure about their married life and delay having kids if they live in a rented home, since they may be forced to move out when the contract can't be renewed.

我認為那像是愛情與承諾的象徵。對結了婚的夫妻而言，擁有自己的房子意味著擁有能專注在彼此身上的私人場所。如果住在租的房子裡，他們可能會對婚姻生活感覺不安全，並且延後生小孩，因為租約無法續約時可能被迫搬走。

### 回答範例 B

Most women don't like the idea of living with their in-laws. With in-laws at home, they may not be able to spend quality time with their husbands, and because of generation gap, there may be disagreements about trivial things. Therefore, in order to keep a distance, a couple would need their own home, which also symbolizes independence.

大部分的女性不喜歡和對方家人住在一起。家裡有對方的家人，女方可能就沒辦法和丈夫度過有品質的時間，而且因為世代差異的關係，可能會對於小事意見不合。所以，為了保持距離，夫妻需要自己的房子，這也象徵著獨立。

|單字片語| insecure [ˌɪnsɪˋkjʊr] adj. 不安全的，不牢靠的 / in-law [ˋɪnˏlɔ] n. 姻親（因為結婚而成為親戚的對方家人，主要包括公公、婆婆、岳父、岳母、小姑、小舅等等）/ generation gap 世代差異，代溝 / disagreement [ˌdɪsəˋgrimənt] n. 意見不合，爭吵 / trivial [ˋtrɪvɪəl] adj. 瑣碎的

## 6　If you had an opportunity to go back in time, would you change anything in your life?
**如果你有機會回到過去，你會改變人生中的事情嗎？**

### 答題策略

對於這一題，採取肯定的回答應該是比較簡單的，你可以回想人生中曾經後悔過的事，並且說如果回到當時的話，你會採取什麼不同的行動。如果是否定的回答，除了對於「為什麼不必改變過去」進行抽象的討論以外，也可以說自己覺得當下的生活比較重要，對現在的生活感到幸福就足夠了。

回答範例 A

Though I don't believe that would happen, I would definitely take the chance to turn my life around. I didn't do well in university, so if I had another chance, I would study harder to get better grades. In that way, I might be able to do a graduate program abroad. That would make me more competitive in the job market.

雖然我不相信那會發生，但我絕對會利用這個機會來翻轉我的人生。我大學表現不好，所以如果我有再一次機會的話，我會更努力讀書來獲得比較好的成績。那樣的話，我或許能在國外就讀研究所學程。那樣會讓我在就業市場上更有競爭力。

回答範例 B

Definitely not. I'm afraid if I made some change in the past, the ripple effects of that change would create a totally different future. What if it turns out the situation is made even worse? In fact, even though we can't change the mistakes we've made in the past, we can still learn from them and try to improve ourselves.

絕對不會。我怕如果自己在過去做了什麼改變，這項改變的漣漪效應會創造出完全不同的未來。要是結果情況被搞得更糟怎麼辦？事實上，儘管我們不能改變過去犯的錯誤，我們還是能從錯誤中學習，並且試圖改進自己。

|單字片語| **graduate program** 研究所學程 / **ripple effect** 漣漪效應

## 7 What are the advantages and risks of running your own business?

**經營自己的事業有什麼好處和風險？**

答題策略

1. 自己當老闆的好處是沒有上司、工作時間自由（free working hours），還有可能賺大錢。不過壓力也很大，如果失敗就有可能負債累累（get deeply in debt）。

2. 如果還有時間，你可以談談如果你自己當老闆，想要從事什麼行業。或者你的親戚有自己的事業，你也可以說自己在他身上觀察到什麼。

回答範例 A

I remember a quote that says, "the higher the risks, the bigger the rewards." Running your own business can be very rewarding financially. Most wealthy people own a business. The possible risks include cash flow problems and competition. If you are in a cut-throat market where price is critical, it can be hard to make a profit.

我記得有句話說「高風險高報酬」。經營自己的事業可能會有很高的金錢收益。大部分的有錢人都擁有自己的事業。可能的風險包括現金流量問題和競爭。如果你處於價格非常重要的競爭市場，可能很難獲利。

回答範例 B

I'm not exactly sure. If you work for a company, you get your pay on time, and you don't have to worry about costs or profits. If you own your business, you need to borrow money from the bank. If the business fails, you'll be in debt. On the other hand, if your business is successful, you can make more money than being an employee.

我不太確定。如果你在公司工作，你會準時領到薪水，也不用擔心成本或利潤。如果你擁有自己的事業，就需要跟銀行借錢。如果事業失敗就會負債。另一方面，如果你的事業成功，就可以賺到比當員工更多的錢。

|單字片語| **quote** [kwot] n. 引用的語句 / **rewarding** [rɪˋwɔrdɪŋ] adj. 有利益的；讓人感覺有收穫的 / **cash flow** 現金流量 / **cut-throat** adj. 競爭激烈的 / **in debt** 負債的

8 Do you think qualifications are important in terms of career advancement and promotion?

**你認為能力資格對於職業發展和升職重要嗎？**

答題策略

1. 在升遷方面，學歷的確是很重要的。你可以引述自己或某個長輩的例子，因為學習不足錯過了升遷的機會。反之，有些老闆或企業會覺得經驗、態度、能力比學歷來得更重要。

2. 在這個人人都是大學生的年代，證照似乎比大學學歷更加重要。你可以說這就是你考 GEPT 測驗的原因。

回答範例 A

Based on my personal experience, qualifications are extremely important. One of my friends is a dedicated worker. He contributed to the company in many ways. However, he didn't go to college. The company promoted someone else with a college degree. My friend was so disappointed that he decided to attend night school.

根據我的個人經驗，能力資格非常重要。我有個朋友很投入自己的工作。他在許多方面對公司做出貢獻。不過，他沒上大學。那間公司升了其他有大學學位的人。我朋友很失望，就決定去上夜校。

回答範例 B

In the case of Taiwan, I think paper qualifications are not as valuable as they used to be. Come on. Almost everyone has a college degree. Ability and positive attitude are much more important. I'm sure the boss will promote someone who is responsible and competent. In short, qualifications are no longer a guarantee of career advancement.

以台灣的情況而言，我認為紙本證書不像以前那麼有價值了。拜託，幾乎每個人都有大學學位。能力和積極的態度重要多了。我相信老闆會讓負責而且有能力的人升職。

簡單來説，能力資格不再是職業發展的保證了。

請看照片,用 30 秒的時間思考以下問題,然後用 1 分半的時間錄下你的回答。

1. Where was this picture probably taken? What makes you think so?
2. What are the people at the bottom of the picture doing? Have you ever seen such a scene in person or on the media? Tell me about your experience.
3. Why is this kind of action popular in similar occasions?
4. Do you think you would enjoy a night at such an occasion? Please explain.
5. If you still have time, please describe the picture in as much detail as you can.

1. 這張照片可能是在哪裡拍的?為什麼你這麼認為?
2. 照片下面的人在做什麼?你曾經親自或者在媒體上看過這個景象嗎?告訴我你的經驗。
3. 為什麼這種行為在類似的場合很流行?
4. 你認為你會喜歡在這樣的場合度過一晚嗎?請說明。
5. 如果你還有時間,請盡量詳細描述這張照片。

1. 從舞台猜測拍攝的現場
2. 說明照片中正在發生的事情
3. 描述圖中人物的心情
4. 對於觀眾的穿著和年齡做出觀察
5. 敘述自己的個人經驗和看法

## 重點補充

在演唱會眾人合力把一個人舉起來，一個接一個把他「傳來傳去」，英文稱為 crowd surfing，而從台上跳向觀眾稱為 stage diving，但不是每個人都知道這些詞，所以你可以用說明的方式描述：a man was lifted up by a few people and passed on to the people behind（一個男人被幾個人抬起來，然後傳給後面的人）。你也可以說這有點難說明：This is a little hard to explain. I wonder if there is a term for it.（這個有點難解釋。我不知道這有沒有專門的用語。）不管怎樣，都不要被「他們在做什麼」這個問題卡住了，因為重點並不在於你知不知道這個詞，而是你能不能確實描述照片中的情況。

## 回答範例

Oh my. This is what I always wanted people to do to me, to be lifted up in the air by a crowd. I've seen rock fans doing this at a concert broadcast on MTV. It must feel great. I'm not sure if the person being lifted up is one of the band members or just one of the audience. From the way he is dressed, he might be a pop star, you know. If he is, then his fans must adore him like an idol. More hands are reaching out to support and hold him. Crazy stuff like this can happen when you attend a rock concert because music can make the crowd go wild. I can't see the stage clearly, but it looks huge. This concert must have drawn a lot of people. It's taking place in the open air. It's nighttime, and there is no rain, just the right weather for such an event. I went to a live concert in Kenting once, so I've had a similar experience. It feels totally different from watching the event on TV. The loudspeakers are so powerful that your heart literally beats faster. You start clapping and moving your body to the music. Normally, fast-paced songs are performed at the beginning. As the night wears on, musicians may step on the brakes and slow things down a notch or two. I remember holding a glow stick in my right hand, waving it to the right and left over my head. It was mesmerizing. I hope I have a chance to relive the experience.

範例中譯

噢，天啊。這是我一直想要別人對我做的事情，被一群人舉在空中。我在MTV 播放的演唱會看過搖滾樂迷這樣做。一定感覺很棒。我不確定被舉起來的人是樂團成員，或者只是觀眾。從他的穿著風格來看，他可能是流行明星，你知道的。如果他是的話，那他的歌迷一定跟愛偶像一樣愛他。有更多的手正伸出來要支撐他。像這樣瘋狂的事情有可能在你參加搖滾演唱會的時候發生，因為音樂會讓群眾瘋狂。我沒辦法把舞台看清楚，但看起來很大。這場演唱會一定吸引了很多人。演唱會露天舉行。時間是晚上，沒下雨，正是適合這種活動的好天氣。我去過一場墾丁的現場演唱會，所以我有類似的經驗。跟在電視上看感覺完全不同。喇叭很有力，簡直會讓心跳加速。你會開始拍手，並且隨著音樂擺動身體。通常一開始會表演節奏快的歌曲。隨著夜晚慢慢過去，樂手可能會暫停並且稍微放緩節奏。我記得自己右手拿著螢光棒，在頭上左右揮動。那是很令人入迷的經驗。我希望有機會再體驗一次。

|單字片語| **broadcast** [`brɔd͵kæst] v. 廣播，播送（過去式、過去分詞和原形相同）/ **adore** [ə`dor] v. 愛慕，非常喜愛 / **idol** [`aɪdl] n. 偶像（指宗教的神像，或引申為廣受崇拜的人）/ **stage** [stedʒ] n. 舞台 / **open air** 露天，戶外 / **loudspeaker** [`laʊd͵spikɚ] n. 揚聲器，喇叭 / **literally** [`lɪtərəlɪ] adv. 照字面意義，簡直 / **wear on** 逐漸過去 / **step on the brakes** 踩剎車（在這裡是比喻的說法）/ **up/down a notch** （程度）往上／往下一級 / **glow stick** 螢光棒 / **mesmerizing** [`mɛsmə͵raɪzɪŋ] adj. 令人入迷的 / **relive** [ri`lɪv] v. 再次體驗

> 請用 1 分半的時間思考你對於以下問題的答案，然後用 1 分半的時間錄下你的回答。你可以用測驗卷做筆記並整理你的想法。

What may be the reasons that drunk driving increases the risk of fatal car accidents? What can be done to prevent people from drinking and driving? Please explain.

酒後駕車之所以會增加致命車禍風險的原因可能是什麼？可以做什麼來預防人們酒後駕車？請說明。

### 草稿擬定

1. 喝酒後可能產生的後果，這些後果如何增加意外的風險
2. 提出法律方面的措施
3. 提出教育方面的措施

### 回答範例

Drunk driving increases the chances of fatal car accidents simply because drivers under the influence of alcohol are not fit to drive. There is no denying that alcohol affects our judgment and slows down our reaction time. In unexpected situations where sober drivers can react in time, drunk drivers may be too slow when they try to step on the brakes or steer away. Alcohol also makes people feel high, and as a result, they may drive recklessly and violate traffic rules. Drunk drivers are often caught speeding and beating the red lights, which are two main causes of fatal car accidents. It's my firm belief that there should be stricter laws to discourage people from drunk driving. Besides paying a higher fine, repeat offenders must be sent to jail. People will think twice before drunk driving if they know there is a heavy price to pay. Schools should also educate students to be responsible citizens from a young age. Another suggestion is to let first-time drivers who just passed the driving test watch videos showing the consequences of drunk driving. Last but not least, family members should also remind one another to refrain from drinking if they need to drive. On special occasions where people tend to drink, they should take a taxi home or arrange for a designated driver to send them home.

### 範例中譯

酒後駕車會增加致命車禍的機率，就只是因為酒醉的駕駛不適合開車。無可否認，酒精會影響我們的判斷，並且減緩我們的反應時間。在意外狀況發生，而清醒的駕駛能夠及時反應的情況中，酒醉的駕駛試圖踩剎車或避開時可能已經太慢了。酒精也會使人感覺興奮，結果他們就可能魯莽駕駛，並且違反交通規則。酒醉的駕駛經常被逮到超速及搶紅燈，這兩種行為是致命車禍的主因。我堅決相信應該要有更嚴格的法律，讓人們不會想酒後駕車。除了付更高的罰金以外，累犯也必須坐牢。人們如果知道要付出很大的代價，就會在酒駕前三思。學校也應該教育學生從小就當有責任感的公民。另一個建議是讓剛通過駕駛測驗的新手看酒駕後果的影片。最後同樣重要的是，家人也應該提醒彼此，如果需要開車就不要喝酒。在人們通常會喝酒的特別場合，他們應該搭計程車回家，或者安排指定駕駛送他們回家。

[單字片語] drunk driving 酒後駕車（= drinking and driving）/ under the influence (of alcohol) 酒醉 / There is no denying that... 無可否認… / reaction time 反應時間（做出反應的時間）/ sober [`sobɚ] adj. 沒喝醉的，清醒的 / in time 及時 / steer [stɪr] v. 駕駛 / recklessly [`rɛklɪslɪ] adv. 魯莽地 / beat the red light 搶紅燈（趕在剛變成紅燈時穿越路口；run the red light 則泛指所有闖紅燈的情況）/ discourage someone from droing 打消某人做…的念頭 / repeat offender 累犯 / think twice 再次考慮，三思 / designated driver （約定好不喝酒的）指定駕駛

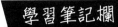
學習筆記欄

☆第一部分：中譯英（40%）

| 等分 | 分數 | 說明 |
|---|---|---|
| 5 | 40 | 內容能充分表達題意，文段（text）結構及連貫性甚佳；用字遣詞、文法、拼字、標點及大小寫幾乎無誤。 |
| 4 | 32 | 內容適切表達題意，文段結構及連貫性大致良好；用字遣詞、文法、拼字、標點及大小寫偶有錯誤，但不妨礙題意之表達。 |
| 3 | 24 | 內容未能完全表達題意，文段結構鬆散，連貫性不足；用字遣詞及文法有誤，且影響題意之表達，拼字、標點及大小寫也有錯誤。 |
| 2 | 16 | 僅能局部表達原文題意，句子結構不佳、有誤，且大多難以理解並缺乏連貫性；字彙有限，文法、用字、拼字、標點及大小寫有許多錯誤。 |
| 1 | 8 | 內容無法表達題意，語句沒有結構概念及連貫性，無法理解；字彙極有限，文法、用字、拼字、標點及大小寫之錯誤多且嚴重。 |
| 0 | 0 | 未答/等同未答<br>*等同未答：例如譯文過短（少於25字）無法評分。 |

☆第二部分：引導寫作（60%）

| 級分 | 分數 | 說明 |
|---|---|---|
| 5 | 60 | 內容妥切表達題目要求，組織完整，全文連貫通順；能靈活且妥切的運用字彙及各類句型結構，鮮有錯誤。 |
| 4 | 48 | 內容符合題目要求，組織完整，全文大致連貫；能正確的運用字彙及句型結構，但仍偶有錯誤。 |
| 3 | 36 | 內容大致符合題目要求，組織尚可，連貫性待加強；能夠運用常用字彙及基本句型結構，但使用較難的字彙或複雜句時常有錯誤。 |
| 2 | 24 | 內容僅能局部符合題目之要求，組織不完整且缺乏連貫性；字彙有限，運用基本句型結構常有錯誤，影響理解。 |
| 1 | 12 | 內容未能符合題目要求，組織不良；字彙有限，運用基本句型結構有許多錯誤，大多難以理解。 |
| 0 | 0 | 未答/等同未答<br>*等同未答：例如 1.文章過短（少於40字）無法評分；2.內容完全無法理解；3.完全離題。 |

| 級分 | 分數 | 說明 |
|---|---|---|
| 5 | 100 | 對應內容適當、切題;說話流利,表達清楚有條理;發音、語調正確、自然;語法正確,字彙使用自如,雖偶有錯誤,仍能進行有效的溝通。 |
| 4 | 80 | 對應內容大致適當、切題;發音、語調大致正確、自然;字彙、語法尚足供表達,對一般話題能應答自如,使用上仍有錯誤,但不妨礙溝通。 |
| 3 | 60 | 能應答熟悉的話題;說話雖不太流利,但已具基本語法概念及字彙,有時因錯誤而影響溝通;發音、語調時有錯誤。 |
| 2 | 40 | 尚能應答熟悉的話題;發音、語調錯誤多;字彙、語法認知有限,語句多呈片段,表達費力,溝通經常受阻。 |
| 1 | 20 | 僅能應答非常簡單的話題;發音、語調錯誤甚多;語法概念及字彙嚴重不足,表達能力極有限,溝通困難。 |
| 0 | 0 | 未答/等同未答。 |

# 台灣廣廈 國際出版集團
Taiwan Mansion International Group

國家圖書館出版品預行編目（CIP）資料

NEW GEPT 全新全民英檢中高級寫作＆口說題庫解析/郭文興,
許秀芬著. -- 初版. -- 新北市：國際學村出版社, 2021.06
　面；　公分
ISBN 978-986-454-159-1（平裝）

1.英語 2.作文 3.讀本

805.1892　　　　　　　　　　　　　　　110007655

## ◉ 國際學村

# 全新！NEW GEPT 全民英檢中高級
# 寫作 & 口說題庫解析【新制修訂版】

作　　　者／郭文興、許秀芬　　　編輯中心編輯長／伍峻宏・編輯／賴敬宗
　　　　　　　　　　　　　　　　封面設計／張家綺・內頁排版／東豪印刷事業有限公司
　　　　　　　　　　　　　　　　製版・印刷・裝訂・壓片／東豪・紘億・弼聖・明和・超群

行企研發中心總監／陳冠蒨　　　線上學習中心總監／陳冠蒨
媒體公關組／陳柔彣　　　　　　數位營運組／顏佑婷
綜合業務組／何欣穎　　　　　　企製開發組／江季珊、張哲剛

發　行　人／江媛珍
法律顧問／第一國際法律事務所 余淑杏律師・北辰著作權事務所 蕭雄淋律師
出　　　版／國際學村
發　　　行／台灣廣廈有聲圖書有限公司
　　　　　　地址：新北市235中和區中山路二段359巷7號2樓
　　　　　　電話：（886）2-2225-5777・傳真：（886）2-2225-8052
讀者服務信箱／cs@booknews.com.tw

代理印務・全球總經銷／知遠文化事業有限公司
　　　　　　地址：新北市222深坑區北深路三段155巷25號5樓
　　　　　　電話：（886）2-2664-8800・傳真：（886）2-2664-8801
郵政劃撥／劃撥帳號：18836722
　　　　　　劃撥戶名：知遠文化事業有限公司（※單次購書金額未滿1000元需另付郵資70元。）

■出版日期：2017年11月　　ISBN：978-986-454-159-1
　　　　　　2024年3月6刷　　版權所有，未經同意不得重製、轉載、翻印。